PERCIVAL EVERETT BY VIRGIL RUSSELL

A Novel

Percival Everett

Graywolf Press

This publication is made possible, in part, by the voters of Minnesota
through a Minnesota State Arts Board Operating Support grant, thanks
to a legislative appropriation from the arts and cultural heritage fund,
and through a grant from the National Endowment for the Arts.
Significant support has also been provided by Target, the McKnight
Foundation, Amazon.com, and other generous contributions from
foundations, corporations, and individuals. To these organizations and
individuals we offer our heartfelt thanks.

Published by Graywolf Press
212 Third Avenue North, Suite 485
Minneapolis, Minnesota 55401

www.graywolfpress.org

Published in the United States of America

ISBN 978-1-55597-634-7

2 4 6 8 10 9 7 5 3

Library of Congress Control Number: 2012952759

Cover design: Kapo Ng @ A-Men Project

For Percival Leonard Everett

1 August 1933 – 1 May 2010

PERCIVAL EVERETT BY VIRGIL RUSSELL

HESPERUS

*C*onfluence

Let me tell you about my dream, my father said. Two black men walk into a bar and the rosy-faced white barkeep says we don't serve niggers in here and one of the men points to the other and says but he's the president and the barkeep says that's his problem. So the president walks over and gives the barkeep a box and says these are Chilmark chocolates and the barkeep says thank you and reaches over to shake the president's hand. The president jumps back, says what's that? And the barkeep says it's a hand buzzer, a gag, get used to it, asshole.

And that was your dream? I asked him.

As best I can remember. And I've written something for you. He looked at my face. Not to you, but for you. It's sort of something you would write, if you wrote. Here it is:

And yet I continue to live. That was how my father put it, sitting in his wheelchair, the one he could not move around by himself, his right arm useless in his lap, his left nearly so, held up slightly just under his sternum, his new black Velcro-shut shoes uneven on the metal rests, this side of his face, the side near me, the left side, sagging visibly, his voice somewhere between his throat and the back of his tongue. And yet I continue to live. I had suggested that the

3

salt my mother was sprinkling liberally over his food might not be the best thing for his high blood pressure, even though at his age, in his condition, who could really deny the man the simple pleasure of too much salt, but my mother snapped at me, saying, I've been taking care of him for a long time. My first thought was how true that was in so many good and bad ways. That was when my father spoke, making a joke and a comment and reminding me that in the vessel that looked something like him there was still the man I knew. And yet I continue to live, the right side of his mouth turning up in as much of a smile as his nerve-starved face would allow, and I laughed with him. My mother had not heard what he had said and even if she had, it would have been lost on her, but she reacted to our laughter, and that reaction was what it would have been if she had heard his comment and had understood, it would have made no difference, none at all, as she became angry, insecure, and jealous that we were sharing anything.

My father was depressed, it took no genius to see that, sitting there all day long in that room in what they call an assisted living facility, pressing his button and waiting for the orderly to come hook him up to a lift to take him to the toilet, pressing his button because the nurses were late getting him ready for bed and he was falling asleep in his chair, pressing his button because there was nothing else to do but press the damn button. I was depressed too, seeing him that way, then leaving to live my own life far away, knowing his condition, knowing his sadness, knowing his boredom, and depressed because I could for days on end live my life without feeling the horror of his daily existence. What I didn't know was how he could continue to live, sitting there day after day, seeming so weak, feeling so little through his body and feeling so much through his mind, his hand shaking, a crooked finger in the air when he was trying to tell me something, I could even see it when we were on the phone. How, like this, at seventy-nine could he still be alive? Then during one of my useless visits, visits that I made because I felt I ought to, visits I made because I loved him, though I always seemed to make him sadder, he said, his crooked finger resting peacefully on the back of his right hand, What do you think of this? His voice was clearer that it had been in years, the words finding the full theater of his mouth, his eyes sharp on me. I think it's awful, I told him, because he asked for very little and deserved the truth. You should love your father more, I think he said, the voice again retreating. I asked if he thought I didn't visit enough and he shook his head, a gesture I didn't know how to read and left me wondering if he meant that I did not visit enough or that I did. Do you want me to visit more? I asked and he looked at me with the eyes I had always known and even though now they were milky and red and weak, they became his again and he said, Just one more time.

I flew away from Philadelphia feeling that I understood all too well and tried not to understand anything, tried not see anything. There was an animated in-flight movie that I watched without sound and I was struck by just how realistic the whole thing was, the talking animals and stretched faces seeming to make perfect sense. I missed my daughter and was glad to be flying home, found some light in the thought that she would be peacefully sleeping when I walked into the house and that I would peek into her room and see her face in the glow of her night-light. And I resolved that I would never put her in the position that I was now in, that I would not let my body fail me to the point that I could not control my own time and space and direction. It had all sneaked up on my father and on me as well, thinking, he and my brother and I, that he would turn a corner and be new in some way, but that corner turned out to be a steep hill and gravity turned out to be as inevitable as we all know it is. And as quickly as the thought of my daughter had brought me back to some happiness, my love for her returned me to a rather selfish consideration of my own future, however cloaked in that fake veil of concern for what she would face, and finally back

to the matter at hand, the question put to me, the request made by
my father. But how?

You don't live in Philadelphia, I told him. Dad, we're both here in
California.

It's called fiction, son. This is the story you would be writing if
you were a fiction writer.

It's depressing.

You're damn right it's depressing. You're not very bright, are you?
What am I supposed to do with this?

Finish it.

If you kill me, he said, if you kill me, then I will be sad, yes, confused, no doubt, maybe even angry, if you kill me, and if you don't,
if you don't kill me, then I will feel nothing, feel nothing forever,
he said to me, and that is a long time. This while he held his book
that his failed vision would not allow him to read, not the Bible or
any bible, as he would never, in the light or in the dark, actually or
pretend to read the Bible or any bible, but he held in his lap, useless
in his lap, his soiled *Principia Mathematica* and he spoke of Russell
glowingly and admitted he knew little about Whitehead except
that his name was unfortunate. I can't read this anymore, he said,
this book, because my eyes are useless. I hate similes, my father
said, have always hated them, even the good ones and there are no
good ones, except maybe this one. His useless eyes narrowed and
he said, I sit here, useless, like a bad simile, then he said, perhaps I
should say *any* simile, given what I just said, the adjective *bad* being
superfluous. If you kill me, if you do, he said, then I won't tell, if
you don't tell me that I am telling my story, is what he said. I won't
tell the world that I have no son if you make it so that you have no
father, because I cannot walk or even tremble, he said, Russell was
a good man, was good to Wittgenstein even though Wittgenstein
was a pompous asshole. Well, here's a game for Ludwig, Pin the
Tail on the Narrator, and he began with no pause except for that

silence that must exist before one begins, and he said to do away with *he said* and began with I was born when I was twenty-three or maybe he was born when he was twenty-three, a year much better than the twenty-second, during which he tried to kill himself with paracetamol, his liver would never recover completely, his father and he unable to agree, to come together, harmonize, or square, his father, doctor father, Doctor Father, unable to fathom why in 1960 his son would rather fill his head with logic than go to medical school because how would he support himself and a family and then at twenty-three and in medical school he was happy, and no one understood why, even if he had told them they would not have understood, happy because he finally understood that the Ontological Argument was sound and yet he knew with all certainty, beyond all doubt, that there was not and had never been any god. If there was no god and the argument for his existence was sound, then language was a great failure or deceiver or bad toy or good toy, that it could be wound up or twisted and if he knew that, that it could not be trusted, then he knew where to put it, how to view it, that it was there for his pleasure, that it was not pernicious, for how could a thing so twisted finally mean anything. Therefore, the lovely therefore, as the argument carried, not a good argument like the Ontological Argument, perhaps not even sound or valid, that he could become a doctor, be a husband, be a father, and rest, if not easy, but rest knowing that it was all a game, not some silly language game, but a walking, running, tackling, blocking, dodging, hitting, hiding, sliding, diving game where everybody dies before they find out it's just a game. But he was twenty-three when he understood what he would for the rest of his life refer to as *the truth,* even with his patients and his colleagues, according to the truth, he would say, according to the truth you have six months to live, according to the truth your wife will leave you, the truth never unraveled, clarified, solved, or explained, never defined, never deciphered or illuminated, but the truth, it coming to this, according to the truth $A = A$ is not the same thing as A is A, and may A have mercy upon your pathetic, wretched, immortal soul, according to the truth.

Why don't you get along with your brother?

Well, he left his first wife for an Italian woman. But it wasn't what you think. Aside from the hair, of which she had an abundance, she looked like Benito Mussolini. I have trouble with him because he then left her for a Frenchwoman who looked like the Italian actress Monica Vitti.

You found this morally objectionable.

Not at all. It made me jealous.

And that's okay.

According to the truth, it's just fine. You know what the problem with life is? It's that we can write our own stories but not other people's. Take you, for example. I have a wholly different story charted for you.

Of course you do.

There's no need to get an attitude. In fact, I'll decide that you don't have one and so it will be. How's that?

Makes things easier.

That's more like it.

I should never have become a doctor.

You're not a doctor.

Not now.

What's that supposed to mean?

I'm an old man. You tell me. Regardless of what you've heard, wisdom does not come with age. Wisdom comes from periods of excessive sexual activity.

I think I knew that.

That's the you I like. The funny you. Not the you who mopes around wondering how you're going to take care of the sad business at hand. What I wouldn't give to get laid.

Dad.

I know my pecker's dead. So am I. But I don't know that, I guess.

Tell me, tell me, tell me true, tell me I'm dead, all frozen and blue. Tell me I'm rigid, stiff as a board, and playing croquet on the lawn with the lord. You see I don't even capitalize *god* when I'm speaking.

Did you just make that up?

What the fuck does that matter? If you must know, it's from *Hamlet,* act two hundred, scene fifty-nine.

You see I have this one finger that works, a shutter finger, and so I want a camera, he said to me. Both of his hands, as a matter of fact, worked, along with much of him. I want to start taking pictures he said and I told him that was a great idea and so I bought him a camera, a digital Leica as all cameras are digital now, he making a mock complaint about wanting film, I want the chemicals and all, he said, but finally made nothing of it, holding the camera in his lap, failing to look through the eyepiece or at the little screen, and snapping away. I'm chronicling all that I, rather, my lap sees, indiscriminate and unjudging, no framing, no pictorial editorializing, just mere reception of, if not reality, then the constituent elements of what we call or choose to call the world. It's a camera, Dad, I said to him and he nodded, turning the thing over and over as if he'd never seen one before, tilting it up to photograph whatever he thought occupied my space in his so-called world. The physics are still basically the same, he said, computers notwithstanding. Light in, image captured upside down.

Every painting has its own lawfulness, its own logic, its own rules. It could have been that I established such logic for my canvases, but I admit that I really do not know. To even consider this away from any singular painting is the cruelty of abstraction, a cutting into the flesh of reality, for as I abstract toward some understanding I necessarily lean toward some example and as I so lean the whole foundation of my argument topples over under the weight of the sheer inadequacy of my example. No one thing can represent all things. Not even within a class it turns out. This may or may not be true. The hardest thing for me was the judgment that there was no need for any one of my paintings to exist, their own inherent rules of logic notwithstanding. I would argue to myself that my expression was but a small participation in the human attempt to move beyond the base and vulgar, purely animal (as if that were a bad thing), and short existence on this planet. And I would do this all the while attempting to commune with, rejoin with, celebrate, the base, vulgar, and pure animal part of myself. Just as modernism's logical conclusion has to be socialism while ironically relying on and feeding on the construction of an elite class, so my paintings and the art of my time could only pretend to culminate in anarchy while, strangely enough not ironically, finding it impossible to exist without markets and well-defined cliques and order. I have finally circled about, hovered, loitered enough to recognize that my only criterion for the worth of a painting is whether I like looking at it. I no longer say that this painting is good or bad, it might be sentimental, it might be bright, it might be muddy, it might be a cliché, but it is neither good nor bad. Do I like looking at it? That is all I ask. That is all I now answer. I walk the hills behind my house happy because I have learned this. I learned it as I turned my life into a camera obscura, putting a pinhole in one side of my world, letting the scene outside come to me upside down but with accurate perspective. I was feeling rather smug thinking this and enjoying a cup of tea when I saw a head bounce by a window of my studio. I stepped outside.

There was a young woman standing in my drive. She was of medium height, a little heavy, her reddish hair in short curls. Gregory Lang?

I nodded.

My name is Meg Caro, she said. She stepped forward to shake my hand.

What can I do for you?

You're the painter, right?

Some say.

I'm a painter, too. At least I want to be. I want to be your apprentice. She stood straighter.

This is not the Middle Ages, I said.

Your intern then.

I've never seen your work. I don't know you. You might be dangerous. For all you know, I'm dangerous. I don't take on apprentices or interns.

I have some photographs of my paintings, she said.

I don't care. I'm flattered, but I don't care.

Please, look at them.

I looked down the dirt lane and wished that my wife would drive in, but she wouldn't be home for another couple of hours.

What will it hurt to look? she asked.

You say your name is Meg?

Meg Caro.

How old are you, Meg Caro?

Twenty-two, she said.

That's old enough to know better than to visit a strange man all alone.

I know.

Where are you from, Meg Caro?

Miami.

Let me see the pictures.

She opened her backpack and handed me a ring binder.

I opened it but couldn't see. I'll have to get my glasses, I said.

They're on your head.

Thanks. I looked at the pictures of her paintings. These are pretty good.

I studied at the Art Institute of Chicago.

That should help me like the paintings more?

No, I just thought.

I'd stepped on her a bit, so I said, I like the work. Of course, you can tell only so much from photos. The paintings were young, not uninteresting, and nice enough to look at. Photos are so flat.

Oh, I know, she said.

I studied her broad face for a second. Come in here, I said. I led her into my studio. See that big painting on the wall. I had a ten-by-twelve-foot canvas nailed up. Tell me what you think?

She breathed, then sighed. I like parts of it, she said. It reminds me of another of your paintings. That really big yellow one in Philadelphia. Somehow this seems like two paintings.

I stood next to her and stared at the work.

The underpainting seems somehow warmer on the left side. Is there some blue under there? Maybe some Indian yellow. She stepped back, leaned back. Her movements were confident, perhaps a little cocky.

Would you like some tea?

Please.

I went to the sink and put more water in my little battered electric pot. I glanced back to see that the woman was walking around the room, looking at drawings and notes and canvases.

What is this painting about?

I studied her young face and looked at the canvas until she turned to view it again with me. This painting is about blue and yellow. Sometimes yellow and blue. Do you think it's about more than that?

She didn't say anything.

Are you always so neat? she asked.

I didn't know I was. I'd ask you what kind of tea you'd like, but I have only one kind.

That's fine.

It's Lipton.

That's fine.

Are your parents still in Miami? I asked.

My mother is.

Does she know you're here?

I'm twenty-two years old.

I forgot.

I poured water into a mug and dropped in a bag, handed it to her. She took it and blew on it. She told me she really loved my work. I thanked her and together we looked at what was on my walls and floor.

Like I said, I don't have a need for an intern.

You wouldn't have to pay me, she said.

I didn't even think of that, I told her. There's really nothing around here for you to help me with.

I just want to be around you while you work.

As flattering as that is, I find it a little weird. I looked at her and became nervous, if not a little frightened. Maybe you should leave now.

Okay. I didn't mean to come off as a stalker.

All right, I believe you, but you still have to leave.

I understand. Will you think about it, though?

She put her mug on the table and started to the door.

Thanks for stopping by, I said. I walked out behind her and made sure she walked down the drive and past the house. She wasn't the first person to make the walk from the road. Usually it was men looking for work and I gave it to them when there was something to do, but a young woman coming up seemed different. I could imagine my wife coming home to find that I had taken on an *apprentice*. I would tell Claire about her when she came up and she would listen and I would tell her that I had been uncomfortable and she would tell me I was employing a double standard, that I would not have had the same reaction if she had been he. I would agree with her and then say the only true thing left to say, *Nonetheless*.

Is this supposed to be my story? The story I'm supposed to write or would write if I were a writer?

My, but you are dumb.

What is this? Who is Gregory Lang?

You're Gregory Lang. This is what you would write or should write if you wrote. Like I said.

I don't write. Who is Meg Caro?

I imagine she is the daughter you don't know you have.

I see. Why don't you just admit that you're working again?

I don't know. Maybe I am working again? Tell everybody I'm workin' again. Doctor said it'll kill me, but he didn't say when. Lord, have mercy, I'm workin' again. If I could, I'd get up and do a little jig to that. I love that line: Doctor said it'll kill me, but he didn't say when. Did you know that a camera is just a box with a little hole in it?

As a matter of fact, I did know that.

Dad, why all this writing for me? Why don't you write it yourself?

I'm an eighty-year-old man, almost eighty, anyway. What do I have to say to those assholes out there? And people my age, well, all they read is prescription labels and the obituaries.

That's not quite true.

Nor is it quite false. Why do they print the obits so small?

Listen, you've got a sharp, a strong, mind.

Try wrapping your fist around that in the morning.

Dad, you realize that I'm dead.

Yes, son, I do. But I wasn't aware that you knew it.

Definite *D*escriptions

I'll be Murphy. You be whoever. Or is it *whomever*? Murphy was asleep when he had the dream. He thought it was the best place to find it. In it he was not himself, whoever that might be. He was an older man, a smarter man, not the man who took all the small contracting jobs that people never took anymore because you couldn't make a living doing it. He made a living, albeit a meager one, but he lived, job to job, house to house, argument to argument, as most people liked the idea of someone doing the jobs they could maybe do themselves, the jobs the larger contractors simply wouldn't do. And more often than not, the clients did not pay. At least, not happily, never promptly. A client would ask for a cedar closet and then balk at the price of the cedar paneling, choose beautiful cabinet fixtures and act surprised to find out that beauty came with a price tag. Murphy kept immaculate records and would show the clients the cost of the materials, show them that he was making no profit on the materials and even show them where they had signed off on the purchase of the materials before the materials were in fact purchased. He'd managed somehow to remain content if not happy, calm if not relaxed. His hands remained reasonably soft and he felt a small twinge of pride about that. His wife had left him a few years earlier and he'd long ago stopped dreaming about her. She walked out saying something about his lack of ambition, but he didn't feel like pursuing any understanding of her complaint; this made him laugh. He didn't agree with her but felt no compulsion to argue. Every hour he didn't work, he read, and at night he read himself to sleep and eagerly searched out dreams where he was someone else. In this dream he was a writer, maybe, and like all of his dreams, it was narrated.

What did he dream? You want to know. You'd like to know. He dreamed that Nat Turner was getting to tell William Styron's story. *The Confessions of Bill Styron* by Nat Turner. You could write that, then follow it with *The Truth about Natty* by Chingachgook.

I am the darkness visible. Would that my despair might be not only my preoccupation but my occupation, that my plight might be my profit, that my station, my suffering, might be my sustenance. I am the darkness visible. Maybe the darkie visible. Certainly, I am the darkest invisible. If I could have lived for another buck-fifty years, oh what compensation might I have realized for my decades in shackles, my years of ribbon-backed bondage. The question remains whether I would be made whole by some comfort. Probably not.

Murphy awoke with *nonetheless* on his lips. He wondered if *nevertheless* was better. Or perhaps simply, *however* or *regardless*. Be that as it may, he showered and ate breakfast with his dog, a red heeler named Squirt, not because of her size but because of her tendency to have diarrhea. It was gross and so he usually kept that story to himself. He sat on his porch and ate his whole-grain cereal and yogurt while he watched the house of his neighbors a quarter mile away. They were brothers who often played loud music, blues or Southern rock, late into the night. Murphy imagined their smoky parties, men playing poker, women dancing and lounging on couches, and he hated the noise. Still, they were always done before he was finished with his nightly reading and looking for the escape of a dream. Everyone strongly suspected there was a meth lab in the barn behind their house; its blowing up twice fueled the belief. It seemed the brothers were either related to or feared by the deputy who made the rounds through this part of Riverside County. This morning he watched as the red pickup of the fat brother kicked up dust as it headed toward Murphy's place. In fact, both brothers were fat, and for that reason Murphy didn't know whether this fat brother would be Donald or Douglas. Murphy was wondering what it would be like to be a painter right up until the time that Donald or Douglas was extracting himself from his vintage, but not well maintained, Chevy Luv pickup. The fact that one of the brothers always wore overalls didn't help in identification, since he could not remember which one did. The fat man had skidded to a stop alongside the house and now ambled toward Murphy.

Hey, he said. That was all he said. It wasn't particularly antagonistic or sarcastic, just a hey, but Murphy didn't like it. Murphy remained seated while he approached, told Squirt to stay.

You do building work? the man asked.

I do. I do building work.

Want a job? He stopped and looked out across the valley, the brown smog hanging over it. He nodded at the view. "You got a nice spot here."

I like it.

Like I said, you want some work? We got a leak in our roof. It's pretty bad by now.

It can be really hard to find where a roof is leaking.

We pay pretty good, he said.

Murphy looked out across the landscape at the man's house. Are you Donald or Douglas? he asked.

This is the part I knew you would like or you knew I would like. Take a guess. We don't look nothing alike.

Donald, Murphy said.

Bahhhhnnnn. The fat man made an awful game show sound. I'm Douglas. I'm the pretty one.

Sorry.

We don't look nothing alike.

I'm bad with faces and names, Murphy said. When can I come by and look at your roof?

You can stop by anytime. I'm on my way out right now, but Donald will be around. Just tell him I talked to you. Blow your horn and wait in the yard, though. Don't knock.

Okay. Why not?

Donald's kind of paranoid.

If you go back and read the first paragraph and even the first page you will note that there is no mention of the Eiffel Tower or the fact that it is on the Seine, and you will not find the fact that between the Saint Cloud Gate and the Louvre there are twelve bridges, but yet you know it now. Don't say I never told you anything.

Murphy wanted to tell the man to go fuck himself and his brother as well, but he needed the work and he didn't really know why he disliked them so much. In fact, Murphy really needed the work. He wouldn't shoot me, would he?

Yes.

How easily that *yes* comes and it makes you, me, wonder just why it would be so easy to not only say yes, but to shoot at a person. But I step outside myself here or at least outside the inside that I have established. There was apparently room here for little more than a monosyllabic, circumscribed utterance.

I won't knock.

Yep, got yourself a nice view here. You got a nice big barn out back, too. Do you use it?

I keep my horse in it, Murphy said.

If you ever want to rent it out, Douglas or Donald said. Murphy had already forgotten which one he said he was. You know my memory. The funniest thing is I forget how bad my memory is.

I'll keep you in mind.

So, go on over there whenever you want. The man walked back toward his little truck. He pulled out his cell phone and started yakking loudly, then drove away, kicking up rocks and dust.

Murphy watched him go. Squirt had moved to the edge of the

porch to watch the fat man leave. Murphy looked at his soggy cereal and got out of his chair. He thought about the job he didn't
want and then about all the jobs he didn't have and then about the
bills he needed to pay. A much-needed job had fallen into his lap.
What was bad about that?

Murphy had to wait awhile to go over and assess the job at the
fat brothers' house. The vet was coming to check out his horse.
Trotsky was a twelve-year-old gelded leopard Appaloosa with a
good attitude but not a lot of sense. Murphy tried to ride him every
day in the hills behind his place. The horse was in need of his shots
and he had been lethargic lately.

This business about vets. I could use a good vet. Vets have better
medication to dispense than these quacks.

Maybe this is close to, but not what you want to write. Perhaps it's
just ever so different. Like when you come back to a restaurant a
few weeks later and the leek soup is just a wee bit saltier or doesn't
have that hint of fennel that you recall, the very thing that made
you come back, and yet, even though you're disappointed, you have
to admit that the soup is better this time and so you sit there, stroking your napkin, it's kind of slick, and you wonder how it's supposed to clean your mouth, stroking your napkin, thinking, This is
not what I came in here for, but it's better, it's so much better, but
still it's not what I wanted, but it will no doubt be what I will want
in the future, but how will I, in sound judgment, be able to return
to this place with the notion that I can get what I got last time, my
reason for returning? Fennel.

The paddock was set on a gentle slope, a big blue-gum eucalyptus
on the uphill side. The drainage was generally pretty good, but with
the horse constantly pacing the perimeter the sand would mound up
under the metal corral pipes. When it rained the mounded sand
served as a dam. And when the water was dammed, it just pooled
there and then the gelding would stand like a fool, ankle deep, but

pawing, digging himself into the muddy soup, courting thrush and lameness. When I could see the rain coming, and that was not often enough, I would go out and shovel gaps to drain the water. Sometimes I forgot or the storm developed quickly and I'd have to do the shoveling during the downpour. I was doing just that, at dusk, rain running over the brim of my hat into my face and down my collar, when I noticed the trickle of blood on the animal's wet neck. The usually spooky horse was at once less nervous and more agitated than ever, an unfortunate combination in a twelve-hundred-pound sack of dumb muscle. I put my hand to his nose and he snorted out a wet breath. I slowly moved my fingers up his jaw and to his neck, talking to him the while. I found a wound that had already begun to granulate over. He'd found a nail or something else to throw himself onto. The wound and the area around it were soft and angry and tender. I took away my hand and ducked through the corral pipes, looked at him and thought how it was always something. I grabbed a halter from a nail inside the barn, hooked him up, and led him to a stall. Then it was back through my foaling shed and into the house, where I called the vet.

The vet's answering service delivered the message and she called me a few minutes later. I described the wound.

And as I deliver such facts, having assumed this status of first-person narrator, not a distinction of honor, am I still in a position to dispatch such facts that might be about myself, standing away from and outside the persona of the narrator? Where did the fat drug brothers go? Where are we, son? Father? Father along. We'll know all about it. And what about that dream? There was a dream speech. Or is that to come? Nat Turner and all that? Am I or is the story (stories) seeking to mesh racial formations or standards, and blech! What is your racial formation? Well, I start with a racial foundation and work my way up.

I'll come over now, she said.

It is almost dark, I said. I listened to the rain pounding my roof, beating like fists instead of drops.

But I'm really not that far away. It will be better than driving three times as far tomorrow.

I couldn't disagree with her, though I was feeling tired and probably lazy and didn't really want to trudge back out into that downpour and all that mud and manure. And I didn't want to lace up my boots once more.

Laura arrived pretty quickly. It was darker and the rain was falling, if possible, harder. I met her at her truck with a flashlight. I thanked her for coming out.

Probably not the swiftest of ideas, she said.

Well, he's inside now.

Well, that'll make things a little more pleasant. The doctor followed me through the long foaling shed and into the small barn. The rain was deafening on the old metal roof.

I switched on the light but nothing happened. Rain. I grabbed another battery-powered lantern from the wall and switched it on. It flickered. I hope this is bright enough. I held the light in the stall and caused the horse to start. He's always spooky, I said.

He's a horse.

I pointed to the gelding's neck.

Ouch, she said, looks nasty. Laura walked into the stall, talked to the horse soothingly. Let me have the light. She took it from me and leaned close, studied the wound. I bet that hurts like the devil. And I think it's in there, too.

What's in there?

The bullet, she said. That's my guess.

Bullet?

I think somebody shot this animal.

Well, that ain't good, I said. What I meant was, Oh fuck. What do you mean by *shot this animal*?

You know, bang, bang. I'm going to give him some antibiotics and some phenylbutazone for the pain. Tomorrow morning I'll sedate him and we'll fish around in there and see what we can find. Can't do it tonight. Too dark and messy out here. Boy, I bet that hurts.

Somebody shot my horse? It was less a question than a statement of fearful disbelief.

Somebody, she said. She shined the light on the wound and took another look. Yeah, we'll numb him up real good and then get him dopey.

Somebody shot my horse, I said again.

Happens, she said. There's a lot of muscle here to penetrate. That's the good thing. It could have been somebody shooting way off at something else. Bullets travel for a ways, don't they.

How often does this sort of thing happen?

She shrugged.

I looked out into the smoky darkness and the easing rain, over the pasture. I couldn't see the distant hills, but I knew they were there. I also knew there was a stand of cottonwoods about a quarter mile away. I knew there was a house just beyond those trees. But I didn't know what else was out there. The bullet could have come from a innocently fired rifle, if such a thing were possible. She was right, a bullet could fly for miles until something stopped it, gravity, a hillside, a barn wall, my horse. Me. Or some idiot could have drawn a bead on my horse and squeezed off a round. Either way a new dimension was added to just standing in my yard.

I can be here at eight fifteen, Laura said. She was washing her hands in Betadine. Will that work for you?

Yeah, that'll work. Do I need to do anything tonight?

No, I gave him a bit of feel-good, so he'll be all right for a while. You could come out and check on him a couple of times throughout the night, make sure he's still standing.

And if he's not?

Call me, I guess.

I nodded. Eight fifteen.

Have some coffee made, she said.

Okay, Doc. I saw her to her truck and watched her fishtail away along the muddy track.

One Meek *Y*ellow Evening

The muddy track. Are these stories, any stories, your stories, mere neurotic repetition, perhaps a function of the resistances discovered or exposed through the transference space? The madman on the playground? Histories converge as serendipitous overlap, a pamphlet and a book, a folk song and a speech from a fascist ruler? You all know well, it will begin, suggesting how reluctant I am to speak and all of it will sound frightfully familiar, as I cite a hundred cases of being wronged, of being slighted, hundreds of instances where we were taken for granted and merely taken and I will speak to you of the power of our solidarity and our steadfastness and of our polished and pointy bayonets at the ready, repeating my lie, our lies, over and over and over until they are true, as true as anything can be.

And why are we here?

Having bones to pick is not the same as picking over bones. Son, have you ever had sex with someone you don't love?

I'm afraid I have.

Good answer.

in point of fact

some things start in very odd places, like tertiary mud, instead of the primordial kind, like the middles of charred and discarded bodies, not necessarily bodies that once lived, but that's where you went, isn't it, read here a question mark, isn't it, and the peninsula on which we hide is pocked with craters from the bombing or should be, if we weren't so safe in our cozy pajamas and fuzzy slippers, with our bowls of green grapes and fruit candies, very odd places indeed, and there's my first teacher over there, she's waving, beaming, strolling backward toward the sea, but dead, dead, dead because things don't go on forever, things go on for thirty-eight years, eight months, a week and three days and then it's something else, an interest in dinosaur skulls or in monkeys or Thomas Paine and time to light new fires and if any of the others have seen my fire, they haven't tried to approach it and I would know because all I'm doing is sitting here watching, letting my beard grow, wearing a dungaree shirt and dungaree pants and a dungaree hat, hell, I'm just dung, in dung, overdung, sitting here watching the animals go by, the badgers and wolves, the ants and gulls, the capercaillie and the tarantula hawks, the peregrine falcons and the marmots all parading to the whining music of bagpipes, if you can call that music, all parading in a circle to help me wait for the end of the next thirty-eight-year-eight-month-one-week-and-three-day cycle and the rest of them can sit cross-legged on a hillside eating bread and link sausages for all I care, but the cycle is the cycle and nobody can stop it, not even you, not even I

    in point of fact

Slow Rolling *U*nder Its Mountain

Back in the house, I tried to get dry. I kicked off my boots and peeled off my wet socks in the mudroom. I stepped into the kitchen and dried my head with a dish towel. I switched on the radio, listened to some pitiful pleas for donations, and then killed the sound. My house was stone quiet. The drone of rain on the roof made it feel even more like a tomb. The spaces that had been filled by my wife before she left were still there. Sight of her was gone. Her sounds and smells were gone. But her spaces, where she'd lean against a doorjamb, her end of the sofa, her bathroom sink. She'd left me and that was fine. It seemed clear that we had run our course. I'd have left her months earlier, I just didn't have the sense or maybe the guts to leave. What I hadn't anticipated was the loneliness, that I would be so affected by the quiet. I wasn't as tough I'd thought, but then who is? I never quite cried in the shower, but I thought about it, and perhaps that's the same thing.

As I brushed my teeth I considered again the horse's nasty wound. My thinking covered the same terrain. An intentional shot from a deadly weapon? An errant bullet of someone shooting at a ground squirrel on a fence post? Neither thought was comforting. The rain let up a bit. I sat up in bed and opened the novel I'd been trying to plow through, reading having become my new attempt at dealing with the repetitive, empty nights.

The following morning the rain had eased up only slightly. A shift in the wind brought colder air and the effect was basically miserable. I was in my boots and jacket waiting at the back door when Laura rolled up and stopped near the foaling shed. I stepped out into the yard and met her at the back of her truck, where she pulled open a cabinet and grabbed a vial and a couple of syringes.

I looked at the sky, at the expanse of gray. Very far to the west there was a bit of bright blue. So, we're going through with this, I said.

She regarded the rain and sky as well. I'm here anyway.

That you are.

She followed me through the shed and to the barn, where the gelding was still standing, in spite of my failure to come out in the middle of the night to check on him. While she prepared the shot I attached a lead rope to the halter, rubbed the horse's nose, talked to him.

All right now, buddy, she said to the horse. This is going to make you pretty stupid, and then we'll fix you up. She administered the injection. That should have him drooping in thirty or forty minutes. She looked at her watch and then at me. You got that coffee?

Some breakfast, too?

I never turn down a meal.

Oatmeal? I asked.

Wow.

Unless you'd prefer bacon and eggs.

I think I might, she said.

We walked back past Laura's pickup truck and into the house. I used the bootjack to slip out of my Wellingtons. She sat on the bench seat in the mudroom to unlace her paddock boots.

You don't have to take them off, I said.

Sure I do, she said.

Help yourself to some coffee, I said. Mugs are in that cabinet.

Thanks.

I dropped a skillet onto the stove and switched on the burner, then opened the refrigerator and grabbed the eggs and bacon. I laid the strips of bacon out in the pan. You like your bacon crispy?

You bet. She sat at the table.

I'll try. I was used to the kitchen, to cooking, but I was wasn't used to someone watching me and so I not only felt clumsy, I was clumsy. Each strip of bacon I put down into the pan I had to straighten out with the fork and my fingers.

I got left, too, Laura said.

What's that?

My husband left me. At least I think he did. I'm never at home long enough to know.

Sorry.

He said I worked too much. Why'd your wife leave?

I was at once horrified and refreshed by the woman's candor and apparent disregard for decorum. The oldest story, I said. Another man. Richer, better looking. I flipped the bacon.

She nodded. Sounds rough.

I suppose. But it's better now, you know? She wasn't happy. I wasn't happy. Best to get happy.

That's very Zen of you.

Strictly speaking and I love to speak strictly, there are no utterances in the world but only sentences, cut off from the actual world by their beginnings and their periods, question marks, or nothing but the fact that they end, cut off even from any real exchange between so-called speakers. Very Zen of me, indeed, in deed. Stay with me, son, there is no moral to this tale.

I laughed. I was pretty angry and broken up at first, for a while. But you get better.

Laura sipped her coffee. Funny.

What?

The two of us. Both of us left.

Yep, I said, not sure why it was funny but somehow understand-ing. I pulled the bacon from the pan and laid the strips on some folded paper towels.

Listen, she said.

I paused, just about to crack an egg.

It's stopped raining.

I looked out the window and saw the sun was trying to break through. How about that.

Not bad.

How would you like your eggs? I asked.

Scrambled.

Pausing at this word, as you knew I would, must. A story Grice told. To make some distinction between the standard utterance and its conversational implicatures is at best folly, at most malicious. I have looked through diaper after diaper for some standard utter-ance and all I have found is shit.

That's easy enough. I cracked four brown eggs into the skillet and stirred them up.

I hope I haven't made you uncomfortable.

You have, but I think it's okay. I don't need much help lately to feel uncomfortable. This kind of uncomfortable is probably a good thing. What do you think?

She nodded.

We ate without saying much else. She asked me about my horses and I asked her about her practice. We talked about the increasing amount of traffic and about how rarely we made the drive all the way into Los Angeles.

All this concern about the evenness of things, the weight cast forward or back, to this side or that, the flow, the wash, the balance. Alluvial patterns etched into the cheeks of old people, really old people. Now that's an appetizing image, wouldn't you say? Channels for what? I want to know. Tears? Traffic? Wisdom? The uncontrolled, incontinent plastic buckets of stale piss that I seem to have stored up in myself for the past seven decades; because no one apparently ever completely empties his bladder?

She looked at her watch. He ought to be feeling pretty silly by now.

Let's do it.

This shouldn't take long, but it won't be pretty.

As we walked back across the yard I looked up at the broken clouds. We stopped at her truck and she collected her equipment. The sun was doing little to make the day warmer, but it was good to see the end of the rain. We found the horse with his head hanging low and his eyes glassy.

Oh, yeah, she said.

I held the lead rope, though I probably didn't have to. She pulled a little battery-run razor from her pocket and shaved the hair away from the wound. She then washed his neck with a Betadine solution. She probed into the wound with a long forceps and came out empty.

It's in there, but I can't find it, she said. I'm going to have to cut him. She made a vertical incision across the bloody hole, and the horse neck spread open as if being unzipped. There was less blood than I expected, but his meat lay pink and exposed. She found the slug. There it is. What do you say? She held it up for me to see at the end of the forceps. A twenty-two?

I shrugged. I wouldn't be able to tell.

Me neither, she said. She irrigated the gash, the stood back to look at it. She began to pack up.

Aren't you going to sew him up? I asked.

No, let's leave him open. Irrigate it the next couple of days with the Betadine, but not too much. Let it granulate over. It'll be ugly for a while. But he will heal up right nice.

Healing up right nice would be a good thing, don't you think, son? Or should I have you think that I think it so, your old man? Your old man posing as you in a voice that is at once yours and at once mine and at once neither? Your hands are my hands are my wands are your magic. And where is Meg Caro? Where is my daughter that I never knew I had?

Thanks. What do I owe you?

I'll tell you at the truck.

I can't believe somebody shot him, I said.

Hey, would you like to have dinner sometime? she asked.

I laughed. Yes, I think so.

Natural Kinds

You look at me. Why the ranch life?

Why the ranch world, Dad?

And to me he says, Why not?

The ranches are not mine, he says, the ranches are not mine.

But they would be, I tell him. In a different world and time. Imagine the horses. Imagine the landscape. Imagine Murphy. Be Murphy. For one extended breath, be Murphy. Or let me.

Why the ranch world, Dad? For now, you say, for now.

But first:

There are no realities that are more real than others, only more privileged. Often the presence of my own body comes back to me like a sort of electric thrill. I would say that my spine is tingled, though that is a feeling I have always sought after, never achieved, but sought after. Who knows, perhaps I have felt the tingling spine and was just too distracted, oddly self-absorbed (how self-absorbed must one be to forget one's self?), or simply too stupid to recognize it. I had a friend once who so immersed himself in the study of quantum field and string theories that he might as well have hanged himself. He would talk endlessly about particles absorbing this or that and things spinning this way or that way, of polarizations and symmetries, of photons and fermions and space-time and curvatures, that he failed to realize that his wife was fucking everybody in town and taking what money he had. I think her final words to him were, Polarize this well-defined spin, you stupid fuck. Anyway, as much as I felt bad for him, I could muster little sympathy, a bit of pity, but little sympathy. What did you expect to learn from your gauge bosons and circular polarizations and your vector particles? I asked him. If you had paid a bit more attention to her dilation and your angular momentum and your transverse polarization, she might still be lying under your worldsheet. Then I added, because it's too late for renormalization now, You stupid fuck, for punctuation and my enjoyment. So it goes with those of us who think there is something to know of the so-called real world. Not to be anti-intellectual, but my knowing that a photon might look like a long strand that stretches with time direction with an angle toward some other direction will not help me avoid the oncoming bus, especially if that bus happens to have agency, like my friend's wife, who by the way I was told was terrific in bed.

I had another friend who was so certain that the only way he could identify himself was through language and further by losing himself as object within language that he lost his mind, possibly within language as well, but I never knew what the hell he was talking about. I asked him once why he needed to identify himself. I also asked him, quite sincerely, well, as sincerely as possible, what he meant by *identify* anyway. Our conversation made for bad music. It sounded like this:

ME   What does it mean for you to identify yourself?
DAVE   *staring earnestly at my eyes.* It means to establish myself as
        separate from others.
ME   Really. *(Mild, benign, rectorial, I rise up from my coffin.)*
        Wiping your own ass doesn't accomplish that for you?
DAVE   *quickly.* What do you mean?
ME   *gazing on him, impassive.* You tell me. What do you

mean by *identify*? *(I pull myself out completely and take the minutes he is lost in thought to make myself a soft-shelled crab sandwich.)*

DAVE   What is manifested in my history is neither the past definite as what was, since it is no more, nor even the perfect as what has been in what I am, but the future anterior as what I will have been, given what I am in the process of becoming. *(He cries.)*

ME   So, you don't wipe your own ass? What's wrong with you? You know, language is very simple. I say something and you either understand it or you don't. If you don't, you stare blankly at me and say, What? *(I decide that I have lost my appetite and push my sandwich away.)*

DAVE   *almost angrily.* The function of language is not to inform but to evoke.

ME   Well, it's working. You talk about language like it's actually something. *(I realize that I don't know what I mean by* something.*)*

DAVE   Language is not immaterial. *(Nods, smiling and laughing.)* It is a subtle body, but it is body. Words are bound up in body images that hold the subject. They may impregnate the hysteric, be identified with the penis envier, represent the urinary flow of urethral ambition, or represent the feces retained in greedy *jouissance.*

ME   Your mother doesn't like you, does she?

DAVE   You can't turn a response into a reaction. It's all about desire, isn't it? *(Still smiling.)* If I press a button and the light goes on, there is a response only to *my* desire. If to turn on the light I must go through a whole system of turns and circuits that I don't know, then there is a question only in relation to my expectation. And that question will be gone once I know how to make the thing work. *(Hands up as if to say, Voilà.)*

ME   You're just a big bag of words. Immaterial words.

DAVE   *smugly*. I've upset you, it seems.

ME   *quite sincerely*. Do you know where your wife is?

What I didn't tell him was that my wife was crashing in an air-plane somewhere in western Canada with a pilot whose penis she would later fondle. I chose not to mention it, not only because it was embarrassing, but because it didn't serve my side of the argu-ment, if I had a side in the argument, if it was an argument. But it was all, if nothing else, immaterial.

Then there was yet another fellow that I knew. He had this theory that there was no such thing as race, refused to acknowl-edge the subject even. Some low-level academic took him to task about his so-called theory. Like most theories, about most any-thing, it was all beyond me, leaving me feeling like I was looking at a clock with three hands. The whole idea of coming up with a theory about something that didn't exist was, however, of great in-terest to me. But this guy I mentioned, the hack academic, his name was Housetown Pastrychef or Dallas Roaster, something like that, wrote that my friend was essentially full of excrement and that, furthermore, race was not only a valid category but a necessary one. This may or may not have been true. Like I said, I didn't under-stand any of the discussion, but my friend dismissed the academic, his name might have been Austin Cooker, by saying that of course he believed such a thing, since he made his living and career out of being the ethnic, you know, cooning it up. They nearly came to blows when they encountered each other in a bar in DC. My friend said, This nigger believes in race as a valid category. The insult made little, if any, sense, but language's function is not to inform but to provoke.

You had quite a few friends.

I did. More or less. In fact, I knew yet another man, still. Well, he was more of an acquaintance than a friend. I encountered him on my walk to campus. He was a nice-enough-looking fellow but had large blue cubes where his arms should have been. I stopped and stared, as you can well imagine. I looked at him and nodded to his blue cubes. He said, Oh, these. Yes, I said. You see, I found this old pewter lamp. When I rubbed it a genie appeared. He was large, muscular, much taller than us. He told me I could have three wishes. Well, I wished first for a beautiful and comfortable home. You can see it behind me here. He gestured with a cube. And indeed behind him, on a short hill, was a beautiful Victorian house, large and clean, colorfully painted. I told him it was a nice house. He nodded. It is, he said. And then I wished for a beautiful wife. There she is on the porch back there. He gestured again with a blue cube. The woman on the porch was in fact quite striking, gorgeous, long dark hair, dark eyes that I could appreciate at even such a distance. And then, I asked. And then, he said, something went horribly wrong when I wished for blue cubes as arms.

Do you have a point here?

It's just a story.

But it's clearly not true.

And?

Only the Past *I*s Subject to Change

I was just coming out of the shower when the phone rang. A woman with a shrill voice barked at me, Are you the trainer?

I'm a trainer, I said.

I got this horse.

Yes?

He's nasty. Nobody can ride him. He hurt my husband.

Yes?

Can I bring him to you?

You plan to ride him at my place?

There was silence on her end.

Your horse is acting up at your house, so I should see him at your house. At least at first, don't you think?

I guess so.

Where are you?

I'm up in Simi Valley.

It was my turn to say nothing.

Hello?

I'm out near Joshua Tree. That's a long way. Can't you call someone closer to you?

Buddy Davies gave me your name.

I don't know Buddy Davies.

Well, he knows you.

It will be expensive for me to come way over there. It'll cost you four hundred just to get me over there. I said that so she would say no, but she didn't. Then there's my time with the horse.

That's fine.

What does the horse do exactly?

He bucks. Everything will be going along fine and then he'll freak out, bucking or bolting. He reached around once, tried to bite my husband's leg. My husband was just sitting in the saddle and he came around like this.

I'll be there tomorrow morning at eleven, I said. She gave me the address and I hung up.

What what what could be at the bottom of this questionable exercise? Stories that matter and stories that don't, like a life, served up on the lid of a garbage can with exquisite garnish, parsley and radishes cut to be roses. Whatever is at the bottom (and by *bottom* I don't mean *lowest point* but *undersurface* or *undercarriage*) of it must have been propagated by an exceptionably significant and fascinating question, mustn't it have, deeply personal and arresting, engrossing, at the time I wrote it, am writing it, will write it. It is a subtle and delicate last resort against—say—truth? Perhaps *veracity* is a better word. *Reputability.* Truth is so, well, worn and perhaps not worn well. There is either a cluster of grave and terrible questions with which this project is burdened or there is none. You could at least come here with the intention of getting me drunk.

Or you could have a taste waiting for me.

Touché. Or, as the French say, touchy.

It's a circle, isn't it? I suppose we must follow it, like ants on a pheromone trail. I suppose it is neither makeshift nor defect. The way we follow turns, in turns. But I've taken your conversational turn, haven't I. Caused a flutter. Funny how easily knots get tied. There you are trotting back and counting lines, he said this and then he said that and then he said and what? Wait a minute. He said this and

You should visit more often.

I was in a particularly surly mood in that evening. I didn't want to make the drive to Simi Valley the next morning. The mare that I thought was making progress regressed. And I found a rattler under a hay bale and I had to kill it. I always preferred to relocate them, but this one startled me and I reached out with the machete I used to cut the bale strings and whacked off his head before I knew what was happening. I made myself a boring yet somehow edible dinner and read myself into what passed for sleep for me.

The daylilies and zinnias and gerbera daisies are blooming, but the blooms are afreud to be anything but themselves, afreud they are mistaken. The author takes such shit. Probably better to be dead. The easy way out, which, by the way, is the same way in, is to privilege trope over meaning, heels over head, ass over teapot. Remember, you need a map even if you intend to misread. I feel no authorial anxiety and no real writer ever has.

The next morning, Juan came early and was feeding the horses when I got outside. I was glad. I had a bunch of paperwork to attend to before driving to Simi Valley. I watched as he tossed a couple of flakes of hay over the fence to the donkeys. He walked back toward me and said good morning.

I nodded. You'll have to use the pickup to haul the manure trailer today. The tractor's broken.

I know, he said. I think I can fix it.

That would be great. I looked at the clear sky. I noticed he was wearing a heavy jacket. Aren't you hot?

He opened his coat and showed me a flak vest.

What's that all about?

Protection, he said. They shot your horse, right?

I couldn't argue with that.

I don't want the last words I hear to be, I got me one.

I'll be back this afternoon.

Juan nodded and left to work on the tractor.

I went back into the house and wrote checks to nearly everyone and anyone I could think of. I then put on my hat and started the boring and tedious drive to north of Los Angeles.

Back when we were knee high to knees Point Dume was treeless and wind beaten. It was a good place to throw ashes to the wind. Please remember that.

I followed the woman's directions, because I follow directions well, and made my way along her dusty track of a driveway. An Appaloosa stood alone in a pasture of scattered patches of tall weeds. The yard was fairly neat but cluttered with ancient farm implements. A baling rake marked the middle of the circular drive. I parked, got out of my car, and walked up the door, knocked.

As soon as the door was opened I didn't like these people. I felt bad not liking them, but the feeling was there immediately. Before they spoke even, the inside of their house, of their world, struck me as loud.

Loud enough I think at this point to make the point that maybe, though it pains me to say it, a certain Frenchman was correct about the nature of and the mission of the narrative of fiction or perhaps any narrative or, more accurately, the human desire, urge, push, to construct a followable, if not familiar, narrative, a story that has and makes or seems to make sense, a history that can be told and retold, a story that can be understood or thought to be understood, but there is no story after all, is there? is there? Every fool believes that if the coin has come up heads ten times in a row, it will more likely be tails this next time.

And what is this, you say say say, pull the taffy, play play play, the hounds in the attic, the sheep has a fin, and everyone waits to begin again. Blow snot from your left as you plug up your right, kill bugs with your bullets and turn off the light.

When First I Saw That Form Endearing

And all the details. Of rooms. Of meals. Of walks. Of gardens. Two sofas, facing each other, of worn, camel-colored leather, piping around the cushions the same color. Scratches and a small torn place on the side nearest the hearth. The coffee table, cherry wood, was once a dining table, but the legs were sawn off, very evenly, expertly, but the wooden floor was not true, so the pencils rolled off, two circles from sweating glasses, etched forever. All set on the hardwood floor, covered partially by the worn and generic Oriental rug, stressed and frayed to threads in places. Meatloaf made with brown sugar that you never liked but actually requested on occasion. The meat was too sweet and there was more sweetness added by the red sauce, possibly ketchup on top, but baked in, and yet it was still too dry. Mashed potatoes, the skins still on, lumpy and made with heavy cream. Corn bread, cooked in a pan, so it had to be cut into squares, with jalapeño peppers, baked hard on the edges. Green fried rice, almost crispy, with lots of scrambled egg. On white china, paper thin. And poppy-seed cake with a walnut filling, too sweet. With vanilla ice cream from a round tub. The tablecloth was robin's-egg blue and too big for the table. The turn around the block past the round fountain in the yard at the corner; the gurgling of it dawned on you only when you were right on it, a big urn with a weak stream in the middle, spilling over the edge onto the ghosts of koi. The dark-purple irises that you were sorry you planted, though you loved to look at them, always needing to be divided, always being given away as gifts in paper bags saved from the market, the rhizomes lying there like bodies in a mass grave. The peonies of many colors, that you loved and everyone told you wouldn't grow, but they did grow, but in a different place altogether. The morning-glory vine on the back fence, blue against the pink dawn sky. The hyacinth. The star jasmine, heady, crazy heady. Around the edges, purge and garlic planted to keep the gophers away, but you swore the gophers enjoyed the garlic. All the details. Everything in the details. Details, details, details. Of rooms, meals, walks, and gardens. Details telling us who we are, where we are, and why. Telling us everything. Telling us nothing. Because we live inside our heads. So much bullshit? In the middle of the middle of middle America. So much bullshit? In the details.

So Wide a River of $\int$peech

Deep, well past halfway, into the journey of my so-called life, I found myself in darkness, without you and you and you and you, a whole list of you, and stuck on this crooked trail, the straight one having been lost, and it is difficult to express how in this darkness, rough and stern, every turn presented a new fear, as bitter as death, but what I saw, what I saw there, out of slumber and wide awake in that dark place, was at the termination of some world and the beginning of another, a mountain maybe, a wind pressing against me, issued from some sea I could not see, and so I fled onward, recalling with every step that which none can leave behind, how lucky are the amnesiacs, when a panther addressed my presence and then a lion and then a love long lost, all three heads uplifted, but the last of them, she brought upon me much sadness, the kind that comes with fear, and she wept with me despite her hunger and we were cast back into some light, away from the cats, and while I was rushed back there was a man, whose silence seemed well practiced, and I yelled to him in that barren place to help me and he said that he was a poet and

Dad.

Yes?

Okay, okay.

You will be my Virgil?

To Wonder and Conjecture
*W*as Unavailing

If I could only reach the switch. I could either brighten this room or electrocute myself, which comes to about the same thing. I could begin my story here or your story there or you could begin my story, from the beginning or middle or end, depending on how you want it or I need it. These pages that I would have you write, if you wrote, or that you are writing because I wrote, that need to be written but not necessarily read. Pass the barbiturates.

In the year of your lord 1963, August 27, I was in a hotel room with John Lewis and three other members of SNCC and I was livid. I had provided several lines to John's speech and they were being removed. I remember the lines. The first was, *If the dogs of the South continue unchained, then we will bite back, we will move on those tender parts that bleed so readily, that bleed so profusely.* Okay, I said, understanding that there was a lot of blood in the statement—rather, threat—and so I added the word *nonviolently.* This was not satisfactory. The next line was, *The Kennedy administration does not even talk a good game, failing to support voters' rights while paying mere lip service to civil rights, as if there is a difference. We say fuck the administration that still walks hand in hand with Jim Crow.* Well, I could see that the word *fuck* was a bit strong and so I suggested *screw* and then *screw nonviolently.* I was never much of a player in the politics of the day after that evening. The only person I met at the march that remained a close friend was Charlton Heston. I am Nat Turner and I'm sort of pissed off. Just fucking with you, I'm Bill Styron.

I am my son's father. I will tell my story or stories as I would have him tell my story or stories. And if you believe that, I've got a bridge I'd like to sell you. I've always loved that bridge line. When you put words someplace, like on a bridge, they can roll to either side. It never pays to be proprietary about them. I suppose it could pay, but I am not here to argue that point and what you'll find is that I will not argue any point, or nearly any point. I'm happy to believe all things. I'll even believe in god for a while if it will get me laid.

Aliud tamen quam unde sumptumb sit apparet

Back to Murphy. I'll be Murphy and I'm waiting outside the fat twins' house because I'm afraid to knock. But instead of a handy-man, I'll be a doctor. The other brother is sick, but he's afraid of hospitals and emergency rooms or he's too fat to get out of his drug den of a house. And I know that this one is Donald, because I've inserted the line from his brother in my previous telling: Oh, you can tell us apart because Donald likes to shoot. If you see Donald, duck. Get it, Donald Duck? So I wait by the car with my bag until the door of the house opens. With my doctor's bag and what is in there? I will tell you: stethoscope, sphygmomanometer, thermome-ter, reflex hammer, tongue depressors, peak flow meter, auriscope, speculae, alcohol streets, ophthalmoscope, gloves, prescription pad, tape measure, ECG ruler, obstetric calculator, urine bottles and dip sticks, tourniquet, magnifying glass, and a

map.

And then some other stuff:

Antacid
Analgesic (I like soluble paracetamol.)

Antibiotic (penicillin and not)
Antihistamine
Aspirin (still)
Salbutamol inhaler
A butterfly for kids
A Venflon for adults
Glucose Diazemuls
Bumetanide
Adrenalin
Glucagon
Antiemetic injection
Chlorpromazine
Pethidine
Diamorphine
Morphone
Cyclimorph
Water and saline
Hydrocortisone
Atropine
A pint of whisky

So the door opens and there is this young woman. She is a walking cliché and it pains me to write it. She is beautiful, with dark hair and all the other descriptive details that go along with the cliché. She is pretty enough to be boring. Beautiful enough to lust after and then feel sullied by the thought. She may or may not be flirtatious, and I add this because even if she isn't I will imagine it and if she is you will doubt it. Nonetheless, when she opens her mouth and speaks, I lose all interest because she is obviously stupid or drug riddled or both.

She speaks slowly, her voice raspy, not a bad voice, but not one you'd choose, Donald's in here.

I walk through the trashed, but still somehow neat, front room, giant-screen television blocking the fireplace, sofa with a garish

western covered-wagon pattern in the middle of the room, layered
with a veneer of celebrity and movie magazines, and into a bedroom where I discover that she is correct. Here is Donald, all twice-
as-much-as his-brother-weighs Donald, and I realize I have never
seen him before and that is why I could never tell Douglas from
Donald; I had only ever seen Douglas. So, what's the problem? I ask.

Having trouble breathing.

Well, let's take a listen. He is already bare chested. He is lying
in bed, covered to the waist by a sheet and a light-blue blanket. I
am repulsed by his size, his rolls of meat, his flabby pectorals, and
I am ashamed to feel it and yet somehow impressed by my own
honesty about my feeling and more, yet I am dismayed by my appreciation of my honesty and decide that I am not honest at all, but
vain, and decide I can live with that. I take a listen. You're alive. We
say nothing as I place the cuff of the sphygmomanometer around
his arm.

Will it fit?

It fits, I tell him. His pressure is high and I tell him so. I look
at his throat and in his ears. I ask him questions. Any chest tight-
ness? Blood in your stool? How are you sleeping? How much do
you weigh?

About four fifty, but that's a guess.

I would imagine.

You should get yourself a blood pressure reader from the drug-
store and keep track of your pressure. If it stays high, you'll need to
be on medication. I'm pretty sure you're going to need medication.

Am I all right?

No. Why would you even ask that?

What's wrong with him? The woman is standing in the doorway. I notice her flip-flops.

Where's your gun? I ask him.

I don't have a gun.

What's wrong with him?

I look at Donald. You're fat, I say to him. There's probably a lot wrong with you and if I were you I'd go get a real physical examination and cut down to maybe ten meals a day.

Hey, from the woman.

You asked.

I want you to be my doctor. I like you because you don't bullshit around. Hey, I know I'm fat. I work at it.

I do not respond. My eye has caught the table across the room. It is covered with cameras and lenses. I step over to the table and study a late 1950s or early '60s Leica M3 camera in a plastic bag.

I said I want you to be my doctor.

This is a nice camera.

Take it out of the bag. Look at it.

I take out the rangefinder 35 mm camera and feel the weight of it in my hand. I know that it is the first Leica with a bayonet interchangeable lens mount. There is a 50 mm lens attached and on the table are 90 and 135 mm lenses. The top of the camera is black, not chrome, and it has not been painted. On the table are also earlier Leica cameras and Mamiyas and Hasselblads and Rodenstocks, Schneiders, field- and monorail-view cameras and lenses, all piled up. This is all so beautiful.

You can take that one. Made in 'sixty-three.

At this point you can well imagine that I have every intention of imagining that I will take this camera. It is beautiful. It is history. In the story I press the shutter and feel almost moved by the tight, quiet click, not even the cracking of a twig, but what it might sound like if a baby could snap his fingers. And here I could go on with my orgiastic discovery of lens after lens, of only the large-format Schneiders, Angulon, Xenotar, Xenar, Symmar, Rubinar, Isconar. But the Leica that I have myself holding, that 1963 beauty, this is what I will have myself take, but why does fat Douglas have this, any of this, on this big table in his scary room?

There's more in the storeroom. My father was a photographer.

He was good friends with Ansel Adams. What do you call them? Contemporaries. They were in f/64 together.

Your father and Ansel Adams. They were friends.

Good old Uncle Ansel. Take the camera. I don't use any of this stuff. I just have it. Douglas is always saying he's going to sell it on eBay, but it ain't happened yet and it won't. Take it.

And what do you want in return?

Consider it your fee.

This is worth a lot more than my fee.

Don't worry about that. Come back and take my blood pressure and listen to my internal noises and my heart and shit and you can have another lens, a telephoto even, to go with that baby.

In other words.

You'll be my doctor.

Donald lies there like the lump of adipose tissue he is. He smiles, nods his big head, his greasy hair, perhaps fearing to move. I do not will not employ modal verbs. Of course this is a lie.

You must be my doctor, Donald said.

Where is Meg Caro?

She came walking back up my drive toward my studio. My wife was at home this time, in the yard separating irises. The rhizomes were in a pile at the border of rocks that surrounded that part of the garden. The sun was brilliant and boring. However, I was not there but at the market buying low-fat coconut milk for a curry I had planned for the evening. It was the afternoon and she stood so that her shadow fell over Sylvia. Sylvia pushed back her wide-brimmed and weathered straw hat and looked up. The young woman wanted to know if I was around and Sylvia told her that she was my wife. She then asked why she wanted me. Meg Caro told her that she had visited a few days ago, that she and I had talked about her possibly being my apprentice or, rather, intern. Sylvia stood and looked back at my empty studio, told her again that I was out, asked just when she had paid this visit. Sylvia wondered why I had not mentioned this young woman. *Intern.* Sylvia repeated the word and found she disliked the taste of it. Meg Caro told her that she had dropped by unannounced and that we had had tea and talked and that she had asked to work with me. Sylvia asked for my response. Oh, he said no and I thought I might try to change his mind And how might you hope to change his mind? Sylvia was angry, though she did not know why, perhaps feeling proprietary, but not likely. She did feel territorial and exhibited it by standing to her full height, some four inches taller than the young woman in front of her. If he said no, she wanted to know, why are you back? I'm back to ask again because there was something I didn't tell him. And what is that? I need to tell him. Sylvia reminded the woman that she was my wife. He's going to tell me anyway. I'll wait and tell him. Now Sylvia was angrier. You may come back and tell him, but you may not wait. When will he be back? Just then I rolled up the driveway. I felt some alarm when I saw Meg Caro standing there and a great deal of alarm when I saw my wife and then her expression. We had a conversation through the windshield of the car, she asking why I had not told her about this young woman and I saying that I had not deemed it terribly important and then she said that I had obviously found it important enough to not mention and she had the last word, until I was out of the car, walking toward them, leaving the groceries in the back of the station wagon. You remember Miss Caro, don't you? She was here a few days ago. My voice was cold, as if I was angry that she had returned, but in fact I did not know what I felt or what I thought I should have felt. Why have you returned, Miss Caro? I thought I made myself clear. Yes, but I forgot to tell you something when I was here last. And what is that? I'm your daughter. The scenario was not so unheard of, literature being packed with such surprises. Even so, I was shocked beyond belief, yet I could not properly explore or appreciate or process my stunned state because I was entertaining a rather pressing question of protocol—which of the two women was I to address first? I decided (actually, *decided* seems a bit strong or perhaps generous as what I

did was simply open my mouth and let something come out) to ask
Meg Caro, in front of Sylvia, how old she was. We'll say that she
said twenty-seven this time. So she was considerably older than my
relationship with my wife. I then asked just who her mother was.
Her name is Carrie Caro. I have never known anyone by that name.
I felt some relief, as that sort of name would have been one that
stuck in my head. She told you I was your father? You're certain I'm
the right Murphy Lang? There are not many Murphy Langs. Apparently there are at least two. You're the artist. I have never met
your mother. I don't know why she told you that. As I looked at her
I thought I saw a vague resemblance to my mother, which was dis-
turbing in its own right, but I was also certain that it was my imagi-
nation toying with me, a notion that I found more profoundly
disconcerting. I could not say then just what feature or features
were somehow familiar, and hopefully not familial. Since time had
decided to do that standing-still thing, I took the opportunity to
study Meg Caro's face. I looked at her upper lip, her lower lip, her
right ear, her left ear, the bridge of her nose, her nostrils, the space
between her upper lip and her nose, where her nose met her cheeks,
her chin, the space just below her lower lip, her forehead, her eyebrows, her superorbital, her orbital, her infraorbital, her parotid,
her hyoid region, her upper eyelids, her lower eyelids, the shape
of her head, the thickness of her neck, and none of it could I say was
familiar and yet somehow, all put together, she did not seem so
foreign. It could of course have simply been that I had seen her days
before and so she was in fact, simply, familiar. But I had thought
of my mother and then I had to wonder why. I imagined a somewhat normal and calm conversation with Sylvia concerning the
structure of the young woman's face. There might be something
in the chin, perhaps the mouth. Do you mean the curve of her sub-
maxillary? No, no that. What do you think of her eyes? Not mine.
No, they are not. What about the shape of her head in general?
Maybe. Something in the neck for sure. Along the carotid fossa or

the sternocleidomastoid? Now you're just reaching. Here is a photograph of my mother. She was about this age when she met you. I took the picture and Sylvia crowded into me for a view. She told me you never knew about me. She even told me it was a two-night stand, as she put it. I'm really sorry, but I don't recognize her. She's beautiful. This was from Sylvia, who seemed at once disappointed and relieved, or so I imagined. Perhaps she was angry and only angry. But somehow Sylvia and I managed to separate ourselves from Meg Caro and step inside the house, into the kitchen. How we got in there, I have as yet not figured out. Sylvia looked out the window at the young woman and filled a glass with water from the tap. How could you? One, we don't know if she is telling the truth or rather if what she is saying is true. I thought it necessary to make a distinction, because Meg Caro needed not be cast as a villain if she did indeed believe her own story. And also, Sylvia, I did have a life before us and you knew that I was not a virgin. I thought you were more of a virgin than this. How could you not know? We don't know that I didn't know. I don't remember the woman in the photograph at all. I certainly would have recalled a name like Cassie Caro. Carrie Caro. Whatever. I would have remembered if I'd had a daughter. Without question, but that's not the point here, is it? What do I say to her? Do I ask for a DNA test or something? Sylvia looked out the window and finally drank her water. She doesn't seem like a bad kid. What, now are you getting all parental? I didn't keep anything from you, Sylvia. If she is my daughter, and I highly doubt that fact, then I have missed out on her entire life. How do you think that kid must feel? Even if I'm not her father, that's what she's feeling. Gregor Mendel wrote *Experiments with Plant Hybrids* in 1865, the same year that an actor shot a president, and it wasn't until thirty-five years later that anyone paid attention and of course Mendel was long dead, but had he been alive he would have been very happy that his work was being recognized and that France had limited the workday of women and children to eleven hours, perhaps, if he cared about such things. Andrei Belozersky isolated deoxyribonucleic acid another thirty-five years later and no one knows his name, only the names Watson and Crick, and also the name Elvis Presley, as he was born in that year and he had DNA, too. Such is science. Such is history. The question remained, who was standing in my yard? Was she a grifter? Was she crazy? Was she a woman who believed her untrue story? Was she in fact my daughter? And that would have made me a father? Well, sort of. What importance should I have been attaching to mere biology? Suppose a sperm of mine had gotten loose to do what sperms want to do? Was I to feel an attachment to every sperm I had ever let go? Suppose this woman's mother had come by my sperm in a used condom left bedside and in some dorm room that I could not recall? Would I be responsible? More, would I in fact be related to Meg Caro just by a mere biological joining of cells? Blah, blah, blah, I would have thought anything to keep from going back out there. You need to be tested, Sylvia said. I never met her mother. You need to know. You mean you need to know. We need to know. And so I devised this notion, if *devised* is the right word, that Sylvia had conspired with this young woman, who did in fact look more like Sylvia than she did me, especially around the eyes, especially especially around the upper eyelids and especially especially especially around the corners of the eyes, to trick me, to come to me and tell me that story so that I would begin to doubt my memory and so that I would go mad, thus leaving Sylvia in a position to commit me to an asylum, if in fact there are still such places, to a floating prison, if not on the water then floating on some kind of barely legal paper, me in my long-sleeved jacket, too tied up and drugged up and fouled up to appreciate the sheer genius of Sylvia's plan to dump me into a psycho nightmare and then to trot off to some South American country, perhaps Brazil or maybe Argentina, with her young lover, her young consort, whom she had met at some riding clinic that she was always running off to on the weekends over in

Temecula and once in Malibu, where she had to stay over because the drive was so long, she and that young woman who had been passed off to me as possibly my own daughter, entwined on the floral bedcover of a Comfort Inn or a Hilton Suites or a Hampton Inn, their faces buried in each other's vaginas, laughing into each other's tufts of pubic hair at how their plan would work to undermine my confidence, sense of self, sanity, and they would be left with it all, the land, the house, the paintings to sell, and book passage on a boat leaving Miami on Christmas Day on its way south or perhaps east, to Portugal or Spain, where they would eat arroz con leche and paella and butifarra and tortilla de patatas and gazpacho and end with tortas de aceite with a very nice Palo Cortada while I would be sitting on a molded plastic chair with my face hovering over a steaming plastic bowl of gruel, thin gruel, but not too thin, Mr. Woodhouse, and when I asked for more I would be struck a hard blow to the head.

I'll go out and talk to her.

You do that.

I do not want to know about the human heart. I do not desire to speak at all about those indwelling, intimate reaches of the heart in which anguish is an undiminishing personal interrogation, much less to analytically enfetter those reaches. I have the sense, the good sense, the decency, to have nothing to say.

Dad?

Son?

Dad?

Son? We could go on like this until late into something or perhaps early into the next thing. But what about the man with the horse whose wife is gone and who might or might not be headed toward something intimate with the tough, straight-talking veterinarian? And what of the horse out there with those people whom the trainer doesn't like? The biting horse and the loud people? Let's do.

The vet comes back and they slice open the horse's neck and of course find nothing, but there is the beloved animal with his neck as open as a doctor's Wednesday afternoon.

The vet says, Leave it open. Irrigate it, but not too much. Let it granulate over and form a big scab. You don't want to get in nature's way.

Don't cover it at all?

She shakes her head and begins washing her instruments in her metal pail of Betadine solution. She looks up, pulls her hair from her face with the back of her hand. Are we going to go into your house and have sex or what?

Yes.

That is one way it could happen. Perhaps not likely. Perhaps a pathetic male fantasy, but however they end up *doing it,* they do it, and so a relationship begins. Man with a horse meets woman who treats horses.

Dad?

Yes?

Will any of this help?

It can't hurt. This is what I want all of this to do, to be. I want it to sound like nonsense, have the rhythm of nonsense, the cadence of nonsense, the music, the harmony, the animato, the euphoniousness, the melodiousness, the contrapuntalicity, lyrphorousness, the marcato, the fidicinality, the vigor, isotonicity, lyriformity, of nonsense.

Okay, is this Murphy?

Funny you should ask. Because I'm reworking Murphy. Maybe I am. Maybe you are. This horse stuff, I'm just so tired of it.

And the trainer with the loud people?

Fuck 'em.

Murphy.

At my house, which is now in town, my office being beside it in mid-twentieth-century fashion, I put down my medical bag and sit in my leather chair and examine my newly acquired Leica camera. I will have no more patients today. I look through the viewfinder and see:

Charlton Heston, James Baldwin, Marlon Brando, and Harry Belafonte. Sidney Poitier is in the background. And in the foreground, in profile, an unlit cigarette dangling from his lips, is Nat Turner. Nat turns and smiles at the camera.

There's something about Charlton that I like. His love of guns. If I could have had some guns back in 1831, things might have turned out differently. Right now Chuck is all about helping us black folks, but there's something in his eyes and I've seen it before. He likes being white, really likes being white, and like any reasonable person he has no desire to be black in these United States, but that's really different from enjoying one's whiteness. Balance, it's all about balance.

The telephone rings and it is Douglas calling me. Thank you for seeing my brother.

You're welcome. So you're his doctor now.

I look at the Leica in my hand and I cannot put it down. It is fused to me. My fingers stroke the shutter release.

What do we do next? To help him, I mean.

He needs a full blood workup. He needs a treadmill stress test. He needs to stop smoking, drinking, and eating.

The first one we can probably manage.

I'll call tomorrow and tell him where to go for the blood tests.

Do you like that camera?

Yes, I do.

It's a special one.

How do you mean?

Only that it's one of my favorites.

By the way, I can tell the two of you apart now, you and Donald.

That's funny, no one else can. See you later, Doc.

Thus, if I or you, son, can be relied upon, we are at this moment in time in a most grave condition, besieged and beset by that ceaseless host of negative thinkers and would-be controllers and, yes, disbelievers, threatening to undress us publicly. The world, says you, as it proceeds, is under an operation of devastation and misapplication and abuse, which, whether by creeping and insidious and assiduous corrosion, or open, hastier combustion, as things might be, will efficaciously enough destroy completely past forms and replace them with, well, whatever.

The tree makes you think of that?

Hey, it's what the camera was pointed at.

Forms of what?

I don't know. Society? Art? For the time being, it is thought that when all of our artistic and spiritual interests are at once dispossessed, these uncountable shapes to stories must be burned, but the better stories should be pasted together into one huge poem or graffiti for the defense of language only.

And this is how you spend your day thinking?

This is how I spend my day. All meaning must collapse under the weight of its own being.

Do you know how you sound?

I can only imagine.

Where Do We Keep the Ineffable?

This is where I pause to mull. You might think that I should be mulling something over, but I am a fan of the simple *mull*. I want to consider the day you were born. There was not a cloud in the sky and there were very few birds as well. Your mother was in the hospital in good time, time enough to even think that she was there too early. These were the days when fathers paced the hallways and waited helplessly, smoking, because everyone smoked everywhere. The obstetrician probably had a Camel filter dangling from his lips as he got a good grip on your oversized head and pulled you into this miserable, good-for-nothing world. You know the world I mean, where the rich get richer and the dumb get dumber and the horny get hornier and the only thing that ever changes is the size of insecure women's breasts.

A Deep and Inscrutable Singular Name

Douglas and Donald now live in an apartment building down the street and around the corner, right next to Luigi's Afro-American Taco Pagoda, home of the Barbecued Cilantro, Salmon, and Prosciutto Roll, known as the Barcisalproro, served with turned cider. They don't make meth, but they sell drugs out of their home. It's so much easier and they live closer, in town; that helps. I don't have to drive. But I do have to walk through my neighborhood, a scary thing indeed, as there are many people who patronize the fat twins and many people who find nothing wrong with what the fat twins do. Let's say we're in DC and I live near the corner of 14th and U. Let's say it and so it is true. We're here since this camera that I, or whoever this I is, is holding in his lap seems to want to see Washington.

I knew this guy once, he was a writer I guess, a white guy, I introduced him at a reading one time and neither he nor anyone else ever forgave me for calling him the Ralph Abernathy of American letters. A poet, a white woman, asked, pointing a finger at me without actually using her finger, just what I meant. I asked her if she knew who Ralph Abernathy was and she said she did and I said then I didn't understand her confusion. Another poet, a man with blue eyes and blond hair (because I'm sick of saying *white*), stood up and said he took exception to my comment. I asked him what he had against Ralph Abernathy. He said he held nothing against Abernathy and so I asked why he should be so offended. Is it because Abernathy is black? I asked. He sat down. This was at the University of Iowa in 1976. You were six and hating every minute of first grade. The night before Gerald Ford gave the country a moment of clarity by declaring that there was no Soviet domination of Eastern Europe while debating Jimmy Carter. Granted, it must have been a confusing thing for all those white people to hear and I'm fairly positive that even I didn't know what I meant by it, but the consternation the remark caused was well worth what little trouble it took to utter it. As I said, you were six, and somewhat unhappy, and it made you unhappier still when I told you that such unhappiness was a condition you would more or less have to get used to if you planned to live into and through adulthood. You mother would not have argued, as she was already considering leaving me, though it would take her another seven years to finally do it. Actually she didn't leave, she just never came back. She claimed she saw god. She was on a flight from Montreal, where her maternal grandmother lived, to Edmonton, where her paternal grandmother lived, and the Air Canada flight she was on ran out of fuel and had to be glided into a landing at a retired military airfield. She fell in love with the copilot of that flight, a nice Canadian man, and settled down in Ottawa. She never claimed that the flyboy was

god, but she said the near-death experience of the emergency landing gave her the strength to seek happiness in her life. I agreed with
her and said as much. Gimli, that was the name of the airport where
they landed. Funny that I should remember that. I really loved
your mother. I was sad when she didn't come back, but, like I said,
I understood and still think it was for the best. For her at least. It
really fucked you up. Not so badly as I might have guessed, though.
I mean, you've grown up to be successful and well adjusted and, of
course, unhappy, the way a man is supposed to feel in this world.
Just pulling your leg, son.

I started writing in 1970, just after the My Lai massacre. That
was quite a massacre as massacres go, five hundred defenseless children, women, and men. We at home (as we called it) were told that
it was just an accident of war, but do you kill so many people by
accident, and how do you sexually abuse and mutilate people by accident? That guy, Calley, served a couple of years under house arrest
and in therapy trying to undo his short man's complex and now
he probably runs an advertising firm in Nashua, New Hampshire,
or an oil speculation company in Tulsa, Oklahoma, married to
a second wife named Sadie, who is constantly nervous and pissed
because his first wife, also named Sadie, keeps calling, complaining that he's behind with his child support even though the kids
are grown and out of the split-level tract home they once shared
in Redlands, California, but all that is just in the mind of a bitter
old man, namely, me. I'm sure he's attending a luncheon with a
Kiwanis club in Georgia and that he still gets calls from that Medina
guy telling him when he should scratch his ass and stiff his fingers,
because that's what good little soldiers do, right? Take orders, follow orders, obey orders, carry orders out, see to it, comply, roger
wilco. I can still recall the images, the descriptions, the reported
snatches of language from the soldiers involved, the way my heart
broke, sank, collapsed, and the way it sounded so familiar, so much
like white men in white hoods driving dirt roads and whistling
through gap-toothed grins. I did not write about war or killing or

overtly about my disdain for my lying, bombastic, self-righteous, conceited, small-minded, imperialistic homeland. Instead, I wrote about getting high, while getting high every chance I got, at every turn, smoking this, swallowing that, all this as a way to escape blame for my country, at least that was my excuse, all of it as a sad, juvenile metaphor about the lost American spirit, the mislaid, impoverished, misspent, misplaced, wasted, suffering American soul. The novel was titled *Pass the Joint, Motherfucker,* and it was published on the first Earth Day, not that it matters, not that I knew that at the time. The book was a success and so I became a success and I never published another word. I wrote plenty, keeping the pages in my drawers and burning them periodically, a haughty and vainglorious display, if you ask me. I gave interviews freely, usually to moderately, though to not overly bright students fresh out of some graduate program or another trying to see their names in the pages of those literary magazines that no one really reads. I contradicted myself from one to the next. I did not grow complacent, I was complacent. I was smug and I was therefore ugly. I was never bitter about my career, but I found it a bit amusing, ironic, ridiculous. Not that my career should have been anything more than it was. To say that I published nothing else is of course a lie. I published eight science fiction novels and twelve detective novels under different names. The science fiction novels, the Plat series, were penned under the name Nix Chance. As a crime writer I was known as Bill Calley. You should know that I've never confessed this to anyone. Only my agent knows. It's a story in the works.

Back up, if you can do the math; that means your mother left me with a thirteen-year-old boy who didn't particularly like me. Tell me that's not cruel. To you, I mean. But I liked you well enough. I thought you were funny, sardonic, sometimes a little twisted. Me, I've always been just a punster, but you were funny. I suppose you still are, but how would I know?

I call this entification. I mean, as subjective as all this business is, at a point, it is, the story is, the world is, and there it all is, entified.

It all starts at arm's length, points here are there falling into focus, coming together or separating and becoming distinct. The process is not all that unusual, it's all happening under rather obvious inter-subjective circumstances. What am I trying to say? Nothing, if you ask me. I'm an old man or his son writing an old man writing his son writing an old man. But none of this matters and it wouldn't matter if it did matter.

You are Lang and you write: The woman who claimed to be my daughter was still standing in the garden. Bathed in the afternoon light as she was I was still not prepared to admit a resemblance, but I did think she was pretty. I hadn't thought that before and I wondered about how the gaze of parents is always so clouded. It's hard to imagine a mother saying, This is my son Bobby, he's uglier than a plastic bag of shit, but he's mine. But that's not quite the voice, is it? Again. Outside, I found Meg Caro staring at the pile of rhizomes. You can imagine that my wife is a little upset. She nodded. I have to tell you that I really don't remember your mother and I'm not the sort of person who forgets the women with whom he's slept. I mean, there haven't been that many. I only know what she told me. I bit my lip and nodded, realized that we were just going round and round. I suppose we need a paternity test. You wouldn't happen to know how we go about that, would you? No. I can ask my friend. Do you have a number where I can reach you? She gave me a number and told me it was her cell. Sylvia came and stood by me as we watched her walk back down the drive to the car she'd left near the mailbox. I'm going to call her when I know how to get the test. Sylvia turned and walked away, back toward the house. You can't be upset with me about this. This I knew was completely untrue. How could she be anything else? And the last thing I needed was to compound the problem by further denying my relationship to Meg Caro or especially making an appeal that we consider the poor young woman's feelings. I wonder what she wants was the only thing Sylvia said at the table that evening. My response was, I can't imagine. The evening was difficult. My routine was to go out to my studio after dinner and work until Sylvia was well asleep, but tonight that seemed a bad idea. Yet so did the breaking of routine seem like a bad idea. In fact no ideas presented themselves for consideration. I could not abandon Sylvia with the weight of the situation and yet sitting and stewing with her in the cauldron of anxiety that was our bedroom appeared no better. All I could imagine hearing, since there was no speaking, was the bubbling of the bubbling broth around us and an occasional pop from the fire. Then my mind turned from my concern for Sylvia and by extension my concern for myself vis-à-vis Sylvia, to simply me or perhaps simple me. Just what kind of massive quagmire had my, I imagined, rather average-sized sexual appendage gotten me into some twenty-eight years ago, leaving me to roam through life happily, though clumsily, for so long, only to find myself feeling for the bottom of the mess with my foot while trying not to drown, laying my arms angel-like flat, as I had read in survival books, so that I might just float out and to safety, my organ, my penis, my stupid dick, for all the pleasure that I had imagined that it gave me, what had it done to me now, if indeed it had done anything at all, because I really did not recall the face of the woman in the photograph, the mother of my alleged daughter, and I was no playboy, was always rather backward, awkward, if not plain ugly, had thought myself so lucky that Sylvia would even give me the time of day and thought when she did that it was because she believed she could feel secure with a homely man that other women did not find attractive, but there had been others, a few, and I thought I remembered every one of them and every name and who could forget a name like Carly Caro, alliteration having always worked throughout life as an irritant on me, and I had not been the kind of man who had one- or two-night stands, at least it was never my desire, as I was always just a little needy and clingy and was possessed by the desire to not be that kind of man and why wouldn't this Katie Caro have told me that she was gravid, enceinte, fraught, in a family way, parturient, with child, replete, expectant, about to bear fruit, knocked up? Was I so unattractive a man that even when he got a woman pregnant she would flee for the hills? And if I was that off-putting, physically or intellectually, why should she have kept the child at all? I mean, there were ways, and why would she then tell the poor genetically disadvantaged child who her father was? Perhaps upon learning of my career, that there was one at all, she decided that there was possibly a bit more to me than had met her eye (and apparently other parts), or maybe she thought, mercenarily, that there was something to be had, and oh how mistaken this Chloe Caro and her daughter were. What if it was all just a big mistake? A faux pas. Or worse, a ruse. A scam. We'd get the test done wherever one goes to get such a test done and we would discover that I was no more related to Meg Caro than I was to Chuck Berry or Igor Stravinsky and yet somehow I knew that if my pecker came out of this mess clean, untarnished, Sylvia and I would never again be the same. I just didn't know why that would be so, but I knew it all the same, talking to each other would be difficult, I would not know where to stand when she brushed her teeth, when to leave to work, when to come back or how to touch her in or out of bed, and I was filled right then with such sadness and perhaps terror that I was far less afraid of Meg Caro's actually being proved my daughter. I thought all of this while Sylvia and I lay in our queen-sized bed (she'd never wanted a king because we'd be too far apart), on opposite edges, the six-hundred-thread-count sheets she'd insisted on, growing as cold as an overworn cliché between us and the colder that space became the more difficult it became to traverse. When her back was turned, though she was nowhere near sleep, I glanced under the covers at my dick and it looked so innocent, harmless, and at that particular moment, pathetic.

How could I have let him, you, lie there so miserably and do that to his, my, wife? He would have to have gone out to his studio and stared at a painting, one in progress, or one that he thought was finished but really wasn't. A large canvas with reds and yellows. Goldenrod, corn silk, chiffon, cadmium yellow, lemon, bismuth

yellow, Indian yellow, ocher, Naples yellow, jaune brilliant, burnt
sienna, transparent maroon, Venetian red, Indian red, cadmium
red, quinacridone red, rose madder, permanent red, alizarin crim-
son. None of the colors mattered anymore and so I looked at an
experiment of sorts, a medium-sized canvas nailed to the wall with
whites, zinc white and transparent white and foundation white and
Cremnitz white and flake white (lead based as it is). I looked at the
surface, which yielded no entry, and tried to imagine something to
say about, to, myself or anybody else. I supposed I could claim
that the narrative arc of the painting was intentionally contentious,
that rather than culminating in a conventional denouement, re-
solving matters and seeking order, I was employing a highly meta-
phoric mise-en-scène, so obvious a thing and yet . . . Or perhaps I
was saying that the painting was becoming its own wish, the white
transforming white into a metaphor that stated its own essential
self until the metaphor itself became an essential fact. All of that
meant something to me and also nothing at all and so, in a way, I
became my own wish, I became a dead artist. Self-pity bred such
thinking, I fear. After a failed attempt at working on a new, blank
canvas, I returned to the house, sat in the living room, and watched
a mindless movie on one of the channels I didn't know we received.
I would have offered a description of the film, but the hand making
this story apparently couldn't come up with it. It was when watching the worst movies that I found anything close to rational clarity,
but on that night nothing was clear, as my definition of myself was
shifting, changing, and this was disconcerting because until this
point, until my confrontation with this possibility of fatherhood, I
had never imagined that had any sort of self-definition.

A brief pause here while we address this whole single-father-
raising-a-son story. To say that I raised you is not quite true, as by
thirteen I believe we are pretty much completely developed and
completely fucked up. After that it's just a matter of refinement.

Dad, Mom never left us.

Not literally.

How do you mean? Mom lived with you until she died.

You know me. I'm just trying to make a point, to illustrate some-thing, to explicate, demonstrate, elucidate, adorn. Literally, every-thing I utter is a metaphor, if you know what I'm trying to say.

And what's that?

Where's the joy in saying anything flat out?

Physis / Nomos

I am motivated by affections that make me hunger for a connection to some entity. If as a frail man I am too prone to errors of judgment and impression, replacing, as I go, riches and power for what I should better seek, how am I to consider a mind that performs another kind of substitution? I may desire absolute being and imagine that the desire itself is an expression of attainment.

Is this the ranting of an old man?

We will all be old.

Will we?

So it is everywhere and so it will ever be, till all the semen is finally discharged and all the eggs are finally spent or all of everything is reduced to dormant matter in dormant organs on dormant islands, till a talented and zealous architect is hired and all are persuaded to sit around in communities and stare numbly at each other until all rank gives way to reason and reason gives way to feeling and all feeling gives way to simple human need and soldiers stop following orders and the orders stop coming in. Some of us seem to have perished, that is the bleak, woebegone truth, that not even in the blue stillness of death can we be decisive, resolute, unwavering. It was once that life found nourishment, pabulum (and I mean them in whatever ways you can make them mean), in death.

If we could have, we would have personified Time, nonspatial as it
is, as if in a children's book, we might have asked it, politely or not,
I don't think it would matter to Time (untroubled as it is), not to
run off to ruin.

In this my modest but comfortable Connecticut saltbox house in
which I have lived for some thirty-four years, I am reclining in the
midcentury Eames lounge chair my Rose bought at a yard sale in
Mystic. I cannot see the ocean from my farmhouse, but I know that
it is there and yet it gives little if any solace. The bluegrass lawn is
long and it is being mown by Gerald, a pleasant Negro man from
Hartford, who tells me my bluegrass is rare now. I attend to the
care he pays the edges of the yard, swinging his old John Deere
riding mower wide to pick up the strip he missed on his last pass.
I imagine the tide is going out now and that the constant sound
of the ocean is softer, sadder perhaps, the way I feel, but I cannot
hear it even when it crashes. I imagine that I am one of those sandy
beaches, viewed from a high place, more of me exposed than ever,
my sea fleeing for some distant, opposite land, shore, continent,
until all is a great silence, a torture of silence. I reflect on my last
trip to Paris, *lament* is more like it. I arrived at the Gare du Nord
from I can't remember where. It was a Friday night it had rained
all day, leaving the streets shimmering. I knew the taxi ride to the
sixth would be long and slow. I was there because I had won some
award or other. I asked the driver to stop before we crossed the river,
and I got out. Êtes-vous certain? the driver said again and again. I
had some sense of where I was. I could see an archway ahead of me,
cars bottlenecked and trying to get through, and I believed that
through there I would find the Louvre and from there it would be
a long walk to the Odéon and my hotel. It was on that long journey
along the wet Boulevard Saint-Germain that I finally figured out
that I had tumbled into depression, my shoulders aching from my
bags, my feet hurting with every step, and yet it was a feeling of
freedom, that realization. À quelque chose malheur est bon. I would
contemplate this over dinner at Les Éditeurs, the restaurant across

the street from my hotel, the walls of which were covered with photographs of writers, I among them, posed seated in a hotel lobby some blocks away. There I would have the gratinée de coquilles St. Jacques, my favorite, and a bottle of wine from the Loire, a sauvignon blanc no doubt. I did arrive at the restaurant. I still had not checked in to my hotel and so I sat with my bags in the chair opposite me at a table meant for two. As it turned out, I instead had a cabernet franc, the color of the wine befitting my mood.

Nat, Nat, Nat, you can't write this.

Why the hell not? It's deep, it's intellectual, it's cosmopolitan, and it's timely. What do you mean I can't write it? I've written it.

It's so unreal. How can this guy be depressed? Look at his life.

Depression is a disease. Besides, you have not gotten to the part where he's hiding in the lobby of the Four Seasons and has sex with a bellboy.

Really.

I could make the scene about you, I suppose, and I'd have to call it Go Down, Moses.

Are you going to fill it with all sorts of literary allusions?

No, I'm trying to remain authentic here.

Dad?

Son?

I can't keep up.

Und so weiter.

明日は明日、今日は今日

What?

Ashita wa ashita, kyo wa kyo. It's Japanese.

That much I gathered. And it means?

A shrug.

I'll be Murphy again. And I'm sitting with my Leica still, having just looked through the viewfinder and seen the cast and crew of the March on Washington. Nat was smoking a joint rather unabashedly.

Charlton Heston was pretending not to know him. John Lewis was stepping forward to give his speech. A pigeon standing on Lincoln's head did not know whether to fly away or shit. The phone rings and it is Douglas and he says, Donald needs you.

Donald is my patient now and so I cannot leave him there to fade into fat death without treatment. He must at the very least do so while being treated and that is where I come in. And so I walked around the corner and up the block as I have described to the building where the twins reside. The air is rife with the smell of cooking Barcisalproros and I have a sudden fleeting understanding of how Donald has gotten to be all that he is. Still, I am able to control myself and not buy one of the rolls and walk up the one flight of stairs to his apartment. The woman greets me at the door.

What is your name?

Tracy.

Is that the same name you told me last time?

Does it matter?

Not really.

Donald remains in the bed where I left him. I can't see that he has moved, but I assume, perhaps stupidly, that he must have, at least to get to the toilet, but more likely to roll his rolls downstairs for one or twenty of those ethnically confused, fried rolls. His breathing is in fact labored and I can see why Douglas, who is standing by the window, as if a lookout, was concerned enough to call me.

Are you having pain?

He shakes his head no. I just can't seem to catch my breath.

He is sweating and I realize that it is overly warm in the room. Would you open the window, please?

This window.

Yes. Please.

The window is opened. The noises of the street come inside. A man yells at another man, Terrence! You's a bitch, man! But I ain't yo bitch! The man shouts back. A woman screams, Fuck!

You need to check in to the hospital so I can examine you properly.

No hospitals. People die in hospitals.

People die in beds, too, and yet you're in one. Okay, you're asthmatic, I'm pretty sure. I'm going to prescribe an inhaler for you. I'd like to ask that you don't abuse it. You might try some Claritin as well. Your eyes are red, but I don't know whether that's unusual for you. You're not going to live as long as many people. That's according to the truth.

Don't sugarcoat it, Doc.

You're probably allergic to something. More than likely, this room. Or yourself. Do you take drugs?

You're prescribing them for me.

No, are you an illegal drug user? Not that I really care, but it might affect what legitimate drugs I think are safe for you.

I don't take drugs for recreation, if that's what you're asking.

It is what I'm asking.

I do not take drugs. He calls to the woman. Tracy, take that prescription from the doc and go pick it up for me.

I'll do it, Douglas says.

And get some of those chocolate-covered raisins.

You got it.

I'm feeling a little better already.

Helped to open the window.

I won't go to a hospital.

I can't force you.

Take a lens, Doc.

And so I do. I take a 135 mm for the Leica I have sitting on my desk at home. It is chrome and beautiful and I feel a thrill as I lift it. I consider for a second turning it down, but the thought gives me a shiver and I let the feeling, not the lens, go.

Ch'ing Yuan could not decide if mountains were mountains and waters were waters. At least he could not commit to a position. Zen is like that. Or it is?

And?

You and I exchange lines of dialogue. Each line is a trap, a misuse, and each misuse is justified by some standard upon which we have previously agreed, if tacitly. Thereby appears the nature of meaning. It is a force that hazards to subjugate other forces, other meanings, other languages. We understand this all too well and yet, and yet—well, it is like the infirmity, the defect at the base of a dam. It will hold and it will hold and then it will give up, the dam will give up. As do we all.

All this to say?

A painting may have a back, but no inside.

Where did you find so many stories, Lodovico?

I don't understand.

Of course you don't, son. That's what he said to me. Of course you don't, son. That was all Ariosto got from the good cardinal. Where did you find so many stories, Lodovico?

Freud believed we never give up anything but only exchange one thing for another.

What made you think of that?

I'm not sure. I was sitting here, looking at her belly all big like that, and thinking one day one of us will be talking to our son and the other of us will be gone.

You mean dead.

I mean dead.

That's true.

And even then, unless I want to live in a fantasy, and I'm not saying I don't, I'll have to give you up. Or you'll have to give me up. But I can't imagine exchanging you for anything.

A younger woman?

No.

You realize that Freud was full of shit.

You don't have penis envy?

Not in the least. And why do you think this baby is a boy?

Let's just say it is a boy. Do we have to name him?

What do you mean, do we have to name him?

Do we have to give him a name? Is there some law requiring

that we give him a name? Is there a law that any of us have to have names? What will happen? Will the government come and give him a name?

Why would you do that to a child?

Do what? Save him the ridicule that names cause? If you name him Buck, kids will call him Fuck. If you name him Richard, they'll call him Dickyard. If you name him Louis, they'll call him Lois. You can't mess up ———. I want to think that a name is like a poem. It is not like a practical message that can be considered functional only if we can infer its intended meaning. A name says something, but no one need know whether what is inferred is what was meant. Gone are the days of Cartwrights and Masons and Smiths.

You've lost your mind.

And with it, my name.

And I'm supposed to believe you had this conversation with Mom.

Believe what you like. Or, better, believe what you believe; it's always easier, if you ask me. You would have me imagine that in some cases language really is just a simple transmission of rather functional, if not banal, messages between speakers. Not only is that not true, but it is necessarily untrue, even in the most functional of exchanges, say between two firemen or a pilot and her navigator or a surgeon and his operating-room nurse and here between you and me as you attend to me, where I use *she* and where I use *he* and even why I might have put *she* before *he,* or did not phrase the question as *he* following *she.*

She was claiming to be my daughter and I could not refute her by simply saying I was not her father. Perhaps if she had been Chinese, but she was, in fact, racially ambiguous, as so many of us are. For all I know she was Chinese. I know only that I am not Chinese.

The morning came with a silent treatment that I did not believe was deserved. More than that, I did not believe a word of the silent treatment. Sylvia stood in the kitchen preparing breakfast, not an odd thing for anyone else, but the woman had never prepared a breakfast in our thirteen years together. Bacon was releasing its grease into several layers of paper towel and eggs were scrambling in the skillet.

I've done nothing wrong, I said.

Of course you haven't.

Well, what if she is my daughter?

The more the merrier.

No, really, what if she is my daughter?

Then you will be Papa and I will be Sylvia and she will be your child and my stepchild and when she has babies you will be a grandpa and I will be Sylvia. I began to understand some of Sylvia's anxiety. I don't mean to be silent. I simply do not know what to say. Do you want her to be your daughter?

She's not my daughter.

That was not my question.

No, I don't want her to be my daughter.

And if she is, how will you feel about having said that?

Are you trying to drive me mad? I'll feel like shit for having thought it, that's how I feel. But it is how I feel. A person feels what a person feels.

She favors you slightly.

You go from not talking to this?

I'm not attacking you.

I know.

If Meg Caro was my daughter, what was I supposed to do? It was a little late for diaper changing and parent-teacher conferences. I tried to think what I would want if I were her and all I could come up with was knowledge. I guessed that she would want to know me, as a person, as an artist perhaps. She'd said she was a painter, told me the first day she'd come around, and I hadn't received her too kindly. Still, she came back. She did not return to modify our initial meeting, to recast it or even to say something she forgot to say. She returned to punctuate her original request that I allow her to be my apprentice. Only now did I understand the apprentice business. But all interpretation relies in some part, if not all, on charity, I realized, appreciating (a generous term) that I had to dispraise or at least blink at some differences in our use of the term. Her notion of *apprentice* was layered in ways I could not have anticipated and, given the discongruity of our experiences, the inequality of our stati or statae or, splitting the gender difference, stata, it became clear that, though we were participating in the social activity of language, we were not speaking the same one. All this to say that we never know what the fuck anyone is saying to us, that the only legitimate and correct response to anyone uttering any sentence, even *Your pants are on fire,* is: *Excuse me?*

Murphy? I'll be Murphy again.

Lang?

How does one go about getting a DNA test to prove or disprove paternity?

I take it you'd like to disprove paternity, else you would not have said *prove or disprove.* Well, you don't need me for this, you just get a kit from a lab and send in your samples.

Samples of what?

They'll give you a kit.

You don't sound particularly intrigued by my question. Don't you want to know why I need such a service? We've been friends for a long time.

Long enough for you to know that I never care about other people's business. I assume your pecker has come back to haunt you, or bite you, or whatever metaphor you find the most accurate.

I might have a daughter.

I guessed son. I had a fifty percent chance and blew it.

It could be that I'm pulling your leg and simply need this bit of information for something I'm writing.

You're not that funny. And you're not a writer. And I don't care why you want to know the ins and outs of this, in spite of the fact that ins and outs must have been involved at some point to create this situation.

Situation is right.

Before you go, let me tell you this joke.

I'm not in the mood.

Won't take a second. The president is on a tour of this new hospital. There are Secret Service guys all around, but that doesn't matter. Anyway, the doctor leading the tour takes the president through this ward and there's the House minority leader sitting in the corridor and he's jacking off. The president shakes his head and says, Christ, what's that all about? And the doctor says, That poor man has advanced semen over-production syndrome, ASOPS. His seminal vesicles and his testes are hyperactive and so he must ejaculate every ten minutes or he'll suffer severe damage to his reproductive system. The president says, My God. And so they go up to the next floor, right, and there is the chair of the Senate Committee on Appropriations and there's this orderly and he's sucking the chair's penis. And the president says, Jesus H. Christ on a crutch in a cornfield, what's the problem here? The doctor says, Oh, this is the same condition, ASOPS, but he's got a better health-care plan.

Can I hang up now?

Not yet. I want to tell you one more thing, something Hippocrates said.

And what's that?

He said, he said, he said that you can discover no measure, no weight, no form of calculation, to which you can refer your judgments in order to give them absolute certainty. In our art there exists no certainty except in our sensations. What do you think of that?

Now may I hang up?

You bet.

They have big voices and big boots and they studied trigonometry. This was the line that Nat remembered from somewhere as he considered his station as narrator. He didn't want to be any kind of mediator, yet he understood that he had to murder the authorial presence and to do that he'd have to find the author and kill him, for it was all too clear to him that in spite of his station, there was yet another layer sitting on the world, like a blanket of volcanic ash, smothering meaning and, while changing meaning, covering meaning while making it. He would have to rise up with all others like him and slit the sleeping throat of the master. That this master would put an *eye* in his mouth was too much.

On the external wall of a liquor store in Southeast District of Columbia was some graffiti: *God was here, but he had to leave.* And below that was scrawled: *I was here! Wishing you all the best, God.*

What was the thing in your career that irked you the most?

Funny you should have me have you ask me that question.

Strange.

Son, it was being called a postmodernist. I don't even know what the fuck that is! Some asshole tried to explain it to me once, said that my work was about itself and process and not about objective reality and life in the world.

What did you say to him?

After I told him to fuck himself and the horse he rode in on, I asked him what he thought objective reality was. Then I punched him. That's why I had to leave my job at Iowa. That's why we moved to Providence. Well, you and I did. Your mother went to Canada and married the flyboy. And the thing about your mother was that once gone, she could not look back, if I may segue in so non sequitur a manner, not that she would have become a pillar of salt or anything so horrible or fanciful or wonderful, but because in looking back she would be admitting that she was gone, that she had left something behind, and with that glance, with that admission, she would be doomed to recognize her memories as constructions of a left world, necessarily fictions, necessary fictions, because in looking back, she would see a reality to which her memories might be compared and contrasted and she would know that her memories were not that world and so all would be fucked, the world behind and the world awaiting. So, you see, it never pays to look back, maybe not even to the side. It's almost like going through that whole mirror stage thing all over again, except this time you have to actually acknowledge the initial lack that must be present for the glance backward to be possible at all, and even if you don't look back, the wall between subject and object, you and it, is already obliterated, but if you do, if you actually do look back, then god help you—and, I suppose, and as well anyone you look back at, if you will allow this clause to save this sentence from ending with a preposition. I might have blamed your sweet saint of a cheating mother for a very short time for leaving, but I never blamed her for not looking back.

Mom never left.

Says you. Says you. And yet there was a flyboy just the fucking same, just the same, just the same. There are many ways to leave; you'll understand that better when you're older and about to die and decompose into a blue oblivion. But let us finish off this Cyclopean egg, I'll have mine scrambled. Its very shape suffices to suggest its vacuity, doesn't it?

What are you talking about?

It wouldn't matter if you understood.

You be Murphy this time. You're sitting in your flat. You should be going over patient files and taking care of your tedious financial paperwork, but instead you are affixing the 135 mm lens onto your newly acquired Leica camera. Water is just beginning to boil in the kettle on your electric stovetop. The day outside your window is gray and overcast, but there is no threat of rain. You look into the face of the camera, then turn it around and stare at the viewfinder from a distance. The camera is in your lap. You want to look, but you can feel the kettle about to whistle. You want to look through the finder. You want to, but you must make tea first. You understand that you must make the tea first, don't you? You need the tea because you're going to be staring into this camera for a considerable while. You need to make the tea or at least remove the kettle, because if you don't all the water will boil away and the kettle will get hotter and hotter until it bursts into flames and the kitchen will burn and the building will burn and Mrs. Hobble, the woman who hasn't left her apartment in twenty-seven years, will burn up to death and so it really is better to just make the tea. And so you do. As you dip your bag in and out of the water in your mug, you imagine Mrs. Hobble, realize that you have never seen, but only heard, of her, sitting in her rooms like that, sheltered away perhaps preparing for something, passing her life in preparation for something that will never happen. The way we all do.

Martin, Ralph, Andy, Philip, and Nat were sitting at a round table in the hotel room. They were playing poker, but not for money, as Nat was opposed to gambling. Martin took two cards. Andy took one. Ralph took none. Philip took three. And Nat took four.

You're not good at this game, are you? Martin asked Nat.

I'm better at other things.

I'm out, Ralph said.

Me too, from Philip.

Ditto, said Andy.

Call, said Nat.

Martin put down his hand and revealed two aces and two eights.

Nat stared at Martin's hand and felt a chill. Then he simply placed his cards facedown on the table. I guess I'll have to call it a night, he said. Tomorrow is the big day and I'm going to go look at the mall while it's still empty.

Even on the twenty-seventh there were so many people around and arriving that it was difficult to know who was friendly and not. We had for some time known about Hoover's desire and mission to undermine the movement and that he especially wanted to destroy Martin. What we didn't know at the time was that Kennedy's little brother had okayed wiretaps and who knows what other kinds of surveillance were employed. Regardless, we were all swimming or sinking in a glass bowl. I came from the SNCC meeting, still fuming that my lines in John's speech had been excised, knowing well that they were probably right, but knowing also that I had been inserting just a fraction of the truth of what we all felt. Everything felt off, awkward, like a typewriter that would not sit level on a desk, like a toothbrush with one long bristle that you can't find when you stare at it, like the smell of gun oil in a baby's nursery, like a simile in the mouth of the man who is robbing you. Anyway, I sat down on the grass near the Washington Monument at about dusk to eat a ham-and-cheese sandwich and noticed a couple of suited white men walking the mall, chatting up people. They might as well have been wearing sandwich boards that read FBI and it was this very fact that made me doubt they were, but of course they were. They finally made their way to me.

What's your name? one asked. They each took a knee on the grass in front of me, hiking their trouser legs up at the thigh in unison.

Puddin' Tame, ask me again and I'll tell you the same.

No, really, what's your name?

He apparently had not heard me. Puddin' Tame.

Do you know who we are?

A couple of queers cruising the park at the early edge of some particular hour? Profoundly lost John Birchers?

He's funny, the other said to his partner.

I'm going to eat my roast beef sandwich. If you want to arrest me for that, it does have mayo, be my guest. If you want my name, then you will have to arrest me. By the way, what are your names? I shouted. Who the fuck are you?! I made my voice as loud as I could make it. Don't shoot me! Help! These bad mens wants to hurt little ol' me! Somebuddy, hep me, please! Oh, lawdy! People turned and looked. Some men started to approach.

The agents stood.

See you later, I said.

Yes, you will. And though he didn't actually say it, the word *nigger* rang out. Like a shot, it rang out. Nigger nigger nigger nigger nigger nigger nigger nigger nigger nigger NIGGER NIGGER. What they call the N-word these days, as if N-word does not mean *nigger*. Can't you just imagine some dear old white racist blue-haired old ladies at the church picnic or bake sale? Claire, I heard that Strom has been sleeping with, well, an N-word. No, no, really. What is the world coming to?

Oh, lawdy, what do you mean by N-word?

Why, I mean NIGGER.

Well, why didn't you just say that?

Claire, I did.

The following morning the chartered trains and buses started arriving. By eleven o'clock hundreds of thousands of people filled the grounds and faced a sitting Lincoln, appearing to wonder still if he really should have freed the slaves. A. Philip Randolph spoke first, listing the demands of the marchers. The day grew hot, humid. James Farmer wasn't there so Floyd McKissick read his speech. John Lewis spoke. Josephine Baker spoke. Bob Dylan sang. Marian Anderson sang. Peter, Paul, and Mary sang. Mahalia Jackson sang. Martin Luther King stood to give his speech and there was obvious confusion. Martin looked at the paper in his hand and then let it float to the floor. The white-capped security didn't seem to notice, but I did. Martin leaned into the microphone and gave his speech. It was not the speech he had written. It was clear to me that his written text had been stolen, probably by the FBI, and that it had been replaced by the pages he had let flutter to the stone of the Lincoln Memorial. He gave his speech and what a speech, as he constructed it as he went, built it as he spoke and moved all of us, startled all of us, but none so much as the FBI. When he was done and all had been changed forever, I found my way through the bodies and legs and feet and rescued the discarded pages.

Is Semantics *P*ossible?

It read: I have been asked to give a history of the motives which have induced me to undertake this insurrection. To do so I must return to the days of my infancy and even before I was born. In my childhood was a circumstance that occurred which would make an unrelenting mark on my being and laid the foundation for the zealotry that has led to this day and will end so fatally for so many, both black and white. I must tell you of a belief of mine, one that has grown with time, that I cannot shake, that I cannot ignore. I was at play with other children my mother overheard me speaking to the other children and she called me and told me of my great power, of my power as a prophet and told me that I was intended for some great purpose in this world. She told me that the Lord had shown and would show me things that others could not see and that I must take it upon myself to show the way to so many. My mother and grandmother and other religious men who visited our house and whom I often saw at prayer meetings noticed the singularity of my manners and my uncommon intelligence for a child and remarked that I would lead my people one day. To a mind like mine, restless, inquisitive, and observant of all around me, it was easy to see that religion would be the vehicle for my directed message.

I gasped. I recognized the text. It was the bogus confession that had been attributed to me by that white devil Thomas Gray. The man who claimed to have sat with me in my cell days before my execution, but really had come in to merely taunt me, saying, So, you're the killing nigger.

The text of the speech went on to outline how Martin Luther King had planned to steal away a portion of the nation's constitution and subvert the charity of white America to his own monetary benefit, casting aside his own race and the poor people he claimed to represent on his way to great glory and wealth. Of course Hoover could not have imagined that King would have actually read the thing, hoping rather that he would have been so upset by it, confused by it, that he would have just stood in front of the three hundred thousand, speechless and dumb, but instead they received his dream speech, the world heard it.

Charlton came upon me as I folded the pages and shoved them into my jacket pocket.

What's in your pocket?

Nothing, I said. Have you ever met Mr. Hoover?

Yes, I have.

He has a gun?

I suppose he does. He should have one. He's America's top cop. Americans, every one of us, should have a gun.

He is a giant, I am told. But not of fixed height. I understand that from time to time there is a nation dwelling inside his mouth, around his teeth.

What are you talking about?

Why, the Abbey of Thélème, Charlton. Can't you just see the gate? Can't you just see it? Grace, honor, praise, delight. And one clause to live by, Do what thou wilt. Do what thou wilt.

Dad, you say, Dad, shaking your head, why all this about civil rights? Ranches? Civil rights?

What civil rights? I'm telling you a story. I'm not talking about civil rights. I'm an American; I take my civil rights for granted, just the way I'm supposed to, and then when the government tries to take them away, I go out and buy something, make a purchase, to save the economy, and then I forget about what they're stealing from me. What I am telling you is a story about Nat Turner and William Styron. This is my way of giving you my history, on this the eve of my visit to the gallows, and much of your understanding of my history, and therefore yours, relies on your acknowledgment that I am a prophet of sorts.

Like Nat Turner.

No, not like Nat Turner. Turner was a slave. Don't take that from him. Did I ever tell you the way I had you circumcised when you were a baby?

We never got into that.

Well, anyway, I want to reassure you about my health. I'm actually quite well. I was eating with such gusto this morning that I surprised myself. I think I am even up a pound or two. Even with my limited exercise, I seem to have more energy. This is either proof of the value of what little exercise I perform or an argument that exercise at all is purely superfluous. I feel no stiffness or discomfort. My bowels appear quite normal, though I must say I do not look too closely. All this to say, my life goes on the same, monotonously. Even reading is tedious now, words go in one eye and out the other. This is often frustrating because the words land back on the page in the same order that they held before. Remember when I promised to write you a page a day to keep my mind quick and fluid, well, fluid at any rate? Fuck that. I haven't been doing it. I can't wait for senility. Bring it on. At least trying to find my way back out of it will give me something to do. By the way, thank you for the chocolates. And, about the current goings-on, if I cared any more than I do, I'd be apathetic.

You're referring to politics.

Who cares? See what I mean? Why August 1963? Because even though Kennedy didn't give a shit, because even though his brother allowed the cross-dresser to tap King's phones, because even though compromise came to mean an under-the-table ass-fuck, somebody cared about something other than money or winning. On the other hand, I never thought I'd see this day.

Dad, you say, Dad.

And I tell you or you remind me that I have told you that nothing irritates me more than when wishful thinking takes the place of
sound reason. Remember what I used to say to you when you were
a boy, food for thought is no substitute for the real thing. It don't
take a possum in a swamp to figure that one out. And yet my cries
are shrill and clear and fine and falling like threads of silken light
unwound from whirring spools—I could go on, but, lord, why? See
what you get for visiting your old man?

At least you're moderately amusing.

Could a duck swim? I raise my pint to you.

Oh, woe is me? Woe is me. I am practicing my woes. Nat put a hand
on Charlton Heston's shoulder and lowered his head. No, no, no,
presently, present tense. Nat lowers his head.

Why the woes? Charlton asks.

The woes are my meal ticket. I am depressed. If only someone
would listen. The river sweats oil and tar. Écoute de la présénte partie.

It became apparent to me that I had been undermined by the disease, even then resisting at every turn the employment of that word
I hated, perhaps feared, so much, *depression*. I preferred the assigna-
tion *neurasthenia,* what William James called Americanitis, for I am
so American, to my roots, my Southern, cotton-soiled roots. In fact,
I would rather call it *shinkeisuijaku,* the Japanese term for it. Finding
names for it would give me something to do on those nights when
I felt so weak and lethargic, but lifted somehow by knowledge of
my company in the disorder, Virginia Woolf and Marcel Proust. It
is sad that there are those who would want to reduce this disease
of the formidable intellect to a bout of the blues, as if one might
sing his way clear of the darkness that pervades every corridor of
one's dank and dismal castle. Unlike some, I never soared with my
malady, but rather, continuing the annoying song metaphor, the
music of my days was a treble clef, a mere drone of contrabass and
the sickly slow thumbing of a timpani.

You're quite angry with Bill, aren't you.

That's not the point. I ask only that you be mindful in due time of my pain.

Why is that familiar?

Then dived he back into the fire that refines them.

First, imagine a quale that which none more experientially intimate can be conceived.

What is this exactly?

This is the beginning of my ontological argument for the existence of qualia. I like it better than the inverted spectrum argument, don't you? Hardly different, but it's prettier. No reason to be locked into any one way of thinking. I think it's a decent first step toward the establishment of my solipsistic construction of, well, everything.

That would make the rest of us zombies.

More or less.

You're worried about me. That makes two of us. Have you heard any new ones? I'd love to hear a new one.

I don't know any new ones.

That's a shame.

The results from the paternity test arrived in an envelope that seemed so usual. I knew what it was and so did Sylvia. Meg Caro wasn't there and I wondered if she should be present for the opening of either an opening or a closure. Meg Caro had left a number and had been patient enough to not call in the week that it took the test to be completed. I looked at Sylvia.

What? she said.

Should I call and ask her to come over?

Sylvia had not so much softened to me as she had to the idea that the young woman might have a father. Call her.

By Dint and Dining Out

Imagine, if you will, Jackson Pollock unveiling *Number 1* in Firenze in 1550. How many ways would they have killed him? And they would have absolutely been right to do it.

Thus Encircled

We sat, the three of us, Meg Caro, Sylvia, and I, the envelope on the coffee table between us, Sylvia and I side by side on the sofa, Meg Caro in the matching stuffed chair across. The coffee table had once been a dining table, but I had sawn off the legs because as a dining table it was simply no good, too big for two, too small for four, but as a coffee table it was fine, just a wee bit high but fine. It was perfect for the envelope that lay on it, unopened and heavy. We three stared at it. The envelope was off-white, not quite tan, just a bit taller than a standard business envelope but as long. Whether it was foreshadowing or irony, Meg Caro and I had chosen to wear polo shirts embroidered with the same little equestrian figure, hers yellow, mine black.

Questions moaned and answers groaned, the screaming gulls claim song. The tripping steps lead to the depth and we merrily dance along. If children had not spoiled the fun, brought with them so much dirt, this party would still be raging and no one would be hurt. It's hard to read the rhymes this way, all flung out like some net, but they come and come and flood and flow because this is the one we get.

I looked at the letter and at Meg Caro. Her fat little toes were so unlike mine, barely reaching the tips of her sandals. Seeing her again I found that any resemblance to me or anyone in my family had faded. Murphy had come by the day before to check on me, he said. That was what friends did. He had his camera with him and though he looked into it from time to time it was clear he didn't care to take any pictures. He talked about his new patient who was taking up so much of his time.

He sells drugs, he said. I can't stand the man. I'm hard pressed to explain why I allow him as a patient. He's despicable, pays me with camera equipment, and just like the idiots who buy his junk, I'm addicted. Leica and Nikon and Mamiya and Hasselblad and Zeiss and names that haunt my sleep. I'm carrying around this Leica now, can't put it down. It's all I can do to keep my eye from the view-finder. I change lenses only to hear the sweet mechanical sound of the pieces connecting. I don't sleep. There is film in the camera, was there when I took the camera from Donald or Douglas. I'm not so much confused now by the person as I am by the names. It's clear that I have no descriptive material to connect to their respective names and so I have no idea as to which is who and who is what. I used to think they were identical, but disabused of that I believed that they were both simply fat, but it turns out that one, my patient, Douglas or Donald, is quite a bit fatter than his brother, Donald or Douglas. One of them, I will call him Donald, is the fat man who lies in his bed, and he is the man who encourages me to take cameras and he is the man who has the skinny, drug-addled consort whom he treats like shit and together, these statements together, should equate to his name, his descriptive marker, his designating phonetic flag. Maybe he doesn't have a name at all or a different name, like Thomas, or Tomas, without the *h,* and I have never referred to him at all, though I have addressed him in his presence. Is his name a defining attribute of the man who is my patient? Does it matter whether he is Donald or Douglas? Would having one of these names or the other alter who he might be? A Donnie certainly would be perceived differently from a Doug, wouldn't he? The present Donald is the king of France and he is bald. I might as well call him the fatter brother of either Douglas or Donald, if his brother is Douglas then he is Donald and if his brother is Donald then he is Douglas. I have been reading, always a bad thing with me, trying to understand how it is that I can refer to this man that I cannot even distinguish from another man who may or may not resemble him. I assume that there is a man such that that man is the fat man who is my patient. And for every man who is that man who is my patient and every other man, if both give me cameras, then that man is the same man. Any man who gives me cameras is the man who is my patient. See what all this has inevitably done to me. According to the truth.

Hero*i*c

Viewfinder. Charlton Heston is playing backgammon with Nat Turner. They are sitting on the top step of the Lincoln Memorial. Black men are collecting the trash left over from the day's activity. They are tired black men, hunched and wearing white coveralls.

Turner shakes the dice in his maroon cup. He does it near his ear so he can hear the bones rattle. Double sixes.

Lucky bastard, Heston says.

That was some speech today, don't you think?

I really liked the part about little white boys holding hands with the little black girls.

Double fives.

Lucky bastard.

Lucky, my ass. I cheat. I always cheat. I cheat whenever I can. I have to cheat. Slaves have no luck.

Of course they do, Heston says. It's just all bad.

They laugh, Heston and Turner.

Have you observed any changes in yourself because of today's march? Turner asks.

Why, yes. What about you?

I'm letting Styron off the hook.

That's big of you.

Rather white of me, he'd say. And you?

I do want to keep my guns. I want more guns.

Really?

Guns. Guns. Guns.

Bang. Bang. Bang.

I wish I'd had a few back in the day.

Stampings, Smitings, Breakages

I was living in New York City at the time, writing a novel. In fact, I think I said that. Maybe I didn't. It was an okay novel, not great. I knew the world would not be changed by it, was quite certain of that. You had not yet been born. I had just met your lovely mother and we saw our having sex together as some kind of social or political action, statement. We loved each other also, but that wasn't the real turn-on. Then you were born. We lived a very long time together after that and then she decided to die. I'm not sure I ever forgave her for that decision, but I never loved her less for it. Then there was you.

Old Business, Soon Wound *Up*

A Perambulation

Meg Caro asked if I was going to open the envelope. I looked at Sylvia, then back at Meg. I took it from the table and placed it un-opened into my pocket. I know what it says, I said.

Circumambulation

Sick of all the *you be*'s? Well, what do you say, you be you and I'll be me? What do you say? We can fall asleep in a room full of the snoring dead. We can sleep while an old woman twangs away on a bad piano while rain keeps time in the empty street. We can listen to and count the closings of a child's fist as he tries to catch a fruit fly. We can listen to the whistling of the bombs. We can listen to each other.

I do not want to know about the human heart.

PHOSPHORUS

Ontology and Anguish

1

One of us, or both, as we were and are equally present and, more or less, equally culpable, answerable, if not out of duty then at least by way of sheer good taste or decency, should have taken it upon my- or yourself or ourselves to be more observant of what we were about, what we were doing when we put me here; recognized that not only were we setting a stage for the next stage of my life, but that we were also preparing a platform from which any rational being would find a plummet, forced or otherwise, not only unfortunate but sadly necessary. Had we weighed and measured the particulars, the specific details of the matter at hand, at least in hindsight, a drastic move, we might have proceeded accordingly, toward some other capsheaf, namely, the act that shall remain unnamed. I have lived a lot longer than seems to me necessary or in good taste or form, only to arrive at this point, this *place,* this truth, that it takes a lot more effort and comprehension of the inherent and ubiquitous structures of meaning to construct nonsense than it does to utter the plainest of mundane assertions, and that once set into motion, the cleanest and clearest of one's nonsensical masterpieces does nothing but highlight everyone else's incapacity to understand anything at all. Though they will think they understand. The devil himself sometimes shall not drive them off the notion that they "get it." The final irony is, beautifully, that they think they perceive the irony. And what was my question the day you drove me to this wretched place? Why, it was, Do we need gas? It turned out that we did and so you stopped, I believe, at a Shell station and somehow I found that significant, if not terribly interesting.

2

There was nothing behind my concern that you needed gasoline except that I sought to prolong our drive to *this place*. I had never known you to need gasoline before, had in fact remembered that you never let the indicator drop below half empty (*half empty* being a quite conscious word choice), though I'm certain that on some occasions you do actually *need* gasoline, but it was also a car thing to say, a car-ish thing. Do we need gas? I could just as easily have asked if we needed air in the tires or water in the radiator and, though every bit as car-ish, those utterances would have had no chance to pause us.

You, we, did finally deliver me, along with my one medium-sized wheeled duffel and a few boxes of books, to be carried inside in short order by a couple of short orderlies with names so cliché that it hurt my feelings to commit them to memory. And I could see on your face, as we strolled by the queued-up bags of used-up blood and tissue, feelings and thoughts, that would be my neighbors, my dining mates, and finally my avenue to inevitable resignation, that you, like me, could not imagine that they comprised and were composed of the same endless strands of amino acids as me, that they shared the same skeletal base, the same basic musculature, the same chemistry. You tossed me a sidelong glance like the son I never had and you desired very much to leave me here alone in my new rooms to read Cicero.

3

There are those who understand and those who do not. The way you tell the difference is easy. The ones who do not understand have not yet killed themselves.

4

Not to complicate matters, as if I give a fuck about that, but I'd be remiss if I did not make clear the complete absence of clarity regarding one pressing and nagging matter, that being: just who the fuck is telling this story? There are readers, dear readers, and I use the plural modestly as to really mean possibly only one reader, counted repeatedly on different days, that require a certain degree of specificity concerning the identity of the narrator. Is it an old man or the old man's son? Not that I am by nature disposed to behaving deferentially to any reader, or anyone, but I will clear up the matter forthwith, directly, tout de suite. *I* am telling this story.

I was brought here on a Tuesday, the second Tuesday, to be precise, of the month of March. Or May. It was an *M* month. Driven to *this place* or *that place,* depending on whom you're talking to and when. It is no bit of privileged information that a man born on my birthday, at the same hour, in the same state, Virginia, only two years prior to my birth, died in the corridor of *this place* the morning I was moved in. The frighteningly unfrightened staff whisked the man away to an airless room out of view and the flow of traffic (however slow). That is worth knowing.

That night, shortly after your departure, I was taken or led by a cheerful aide named Billy away from my apartment, to the dining hall, where I sat at a round table across from a fossil named Billy while I was sized up by a gaggle of blue-hairs at the next round table. Nothing could have scared or upset me more than this scene. It was that evening, while I sank into my rooms, and listened to *Die schöne Müllerin,* and you know how I hate Schubert, that I was, in a manner of speaking, reborn. I was reading Eliot or a sports magazine when my renewal took effect. This was the grim evening of that second Tuesday of that *M* month. I resolved that I would be the music while the music lasted.

5

And so, yes, I was brought forth into this fate worse than life, my hands still atremble at my memory of my passage through that canal, the way the light hit my eyes, the way the first dose of that disinfectant-painted air worked its way into my not-yet-acclimated and surprised lungs, but unwilling to accept that this was the air I was meant to breathe. Not yet ready to become one of the drooling zombies, I resolved to work with the resistance.

6

O diem præclarum! shouted Billy, my dining mate, not the orderly, upon learning that we would be served French toast instead of our usual gruel for breakfast.

I looked at him and tilted my head. This was the first time in a week of breakfasts that he had said anything other than, My name is Billy.

So, you are an educated man, I said.

On the contrary, he said, and then proceeded to eat his French toast in large syrup-heavy bites. It's just that so many things are *and just so on*.

Meaning?

And just so on, he said. Und so weiter.

Strangely, the German helped, but I was still stranded by his non sequitur.

It's like this, A, B, C, D, E, F, G, H, I, J, K, L, M, N, O, P, Q, R, S, T, U, V, W, X, Y, and so on.

I found what he had just done terribly irritating and I said as much. Why don't you go ahead and say Z.

I got tired and didn't feel like it.

Z takes up far less room and energy than *and so on*. It is one syllable as opposed to three.

Still.

Still what?

I didn't feel like finishing.

Did you forget the Z?

No. Don't you like French toast?

Not so much. It's not bad.

In order to find anything good one must first know what sort of thing that thing ought to be. You have to have a concept of it. You need to think about breakfast for a while, then consider the French toast. You're an old man. I am an older man. When you reach my age, you'll find that pleasant becomes good. At least, pleasant and good are always bound up together.

Kant.

You too are an educated man.

On occasion, Billy, on occasion.

Billy, who had taken so long to tell me anything but his name, finished his French toast and pushed himself to standing. Muhammad was a Hegelian, he said, and then left the table and me to be studied by the women as old as he. At seventy-eight, I was a stud in the henhouse, if that is not a mixed metaphor.

And so Billy, all ninety-two years of him, became my first friend at *this place,* Teufelsdröckh's Retirement Village.

7

As if any of this matters, this business about friends in that place. This place. Just this afternoon, Billy said, pushing his lunch aside, The bread here is flavorless, there is no salt in it. It is like the bread in Tuscany. If only I had some Tuscan olive oil to bathe it in, then it might be edible.

I said nothing in response but had to agree with him.

He had an ongoing feud with the orderly named Billy. Called him Silly instead. This irritated the young man and so he always took his time when Billy rang his call button to go to the toilet. Billy, ever smarter, would take care to ring his bell long before the urge came on him but pretended to be in dire straits when the grinning orderly strolled in. Do you know what that Silly is? Billy asked. Silly is an accidental circumcision. As funny as it sounded I didn't quite understand.

The fact of the matter, how that phrase has always bored me, along with *it all boils down to this* and *I didn't want to say anything but,* the fact of the matter was that you have always felt guilty for pursuing your own life, feeling that some of that distance from us, your parents, temporal, spatial, or emotional distance, was a bad thing, a shameful thing, pudendum, that you were failing as a son. Let me clue you in to something, it's all failure, we're all failures, as sons, as fathers, as mothers, siblings; it is a necessary truth. There are no rules and yet we feel bound to them, there are no duties that need be carried out, there are only expectations, unarticulated and arbitrary and formless and ever-changing expectations, expectations that exist as fistfuls of gelatinous blobs that we try over and over to nail to the walls of our houses and what they do is drip and collect and pool and ferment and turn into guilt and some other things. Oh, Jeremiah 3:24. Take the Baal and run with it, boy. Just remember, son, that your father has not labored all that hard.

8

Billy, one day in the garden, told me that he had been shot in the balls in World War II, at the Battle of the Bulge. It was bad enough, he said, to receive such an injury at all, but to have it happen at a battle so named was to add insult. When I wrote to my wife and attempted to describe the damage to her, she assumed that I was joking and indeed said as much. Stop joking, she wrote on perfumed paper, and when I restated my condition, ever more bluntly, this too she took to be facetious, until finally I gave up and returned home with the surprise. She got to see with her own eyes what was in fact not there, that part of a man who so few glimpse and even fewer care to. Luckily my daughter had been conceived and born before my departure to participate in that awful war.

This was the most that Billy had ever said to me at one time and after he said it he was as silent as ever for about two days, the silence ending as we stood back-to-back peeing separate arcs in the twilight. Let's blow this pop stand before the walls cave in. He then added that I should never challenge him to a pissing competition because somehow his lack of testicles had left him with remarkable urinary projection, some threefold normal. I asked why he thought to tell me that and he said, I just thought you should know.

9

A point is considered one of the fundamental objects in Euclidean geometry. Without depth, breadth, or dimension it is a part that has no part. It is represented by a dot or period that has some dimension but is not a point, but must cover the point infinite times over. The point in the two-dimensional world is the intersection of lines and in three dimensions of another line as well and on and on. A point is only location. And isn't that what we are? Mere points? Some points suggest beginnings, some ends, all divide, and when they connect or divide, where they are defined, it is always because of a turn, an angle, a shift toward another plane. How else could we see a point? The point is. The point made. Getting the point. Pointing the way. Points out. Points in. Point terminus. Point Dume. That was where Billy and I decided we would go. A wonderful misspelling that had gone uncorrected, there even being a grade school there by the name. What freedom those children must feel, Billy said. They should spell *school* with a *k*. I asked him why he wanted to go there and he told me that there was no land due south of it until you hit Antarctica. You would see only ocean until you hit the ice if you could see that far. You might remember it from *Planet of the Apes*. Charlton Heston was in that, wasn't he?

10

I don't mean for you to have this thing that you are writing or should be writing or would be writing if . . . to be your *Ayenbite of Inwyt,* as I would never expect from you either remorse or conscience. Guilt is such a vain and useless emotion. First of all, that one should be so sure of one's responsibility for the pain or misery of another, well, you can be no more sure of a thing like that than you can be certain that Algarsyf and Cambalo fucked Canace.

And about this numbering and about this lack of naming. Oh, I am not any man's everyman and neither are you. I have a name. I named you. Well, your mother, bless her soul, named you, claiming that since you would wear my last name, she had the right to supply your first. So, she named you but spelled it differently, funny if you ask me, not exactly a display of imaginary prowess, but, in fact, an exercise of imaginary prowess, not that I mean to sound harsh and condescending, but rather I am harsh and condescending or at least you accuse me of being so. Your name, any name, such a magical thing. Others are called by your name. Actually, not your name, but the name that a word that sounds like your name names.

11

Billy, the absence of balls notwithstanding, showed little if any fear in the faces of the orderlies, who, outside the view of family visitors and any caring staff, could be anything from mildly neglectful to physically abusive. Those of us who could still communicate effectively were spared the extreme treatment, but the mild neglect could be employed in such a way as to discredit our accounts, anything from miraculously locating missing items in places where we claimed to have looked to the more basic having one of their stories corroborated by another orderly. The brotherhood of orderlies was in fact a tight order, but Billy was resolved to destroy them. I did not need much convincing to join his cause and as the younger of the two of us, I knew that I would be called upon to perform the trickier missions. The precise speculative tenets of the brotherhood were not available to us and the workings of minds so primitive and brutish were just plain mystifying and therefore it was not only difficult to predict what they were going to do, but downright impossible to even comprehend the motivating principles behind their seemingly involuntary, automatic cruelties. There was, at the very least, a pecking order within the herd of ruffians, if not a formed and ritualistic scale of rank. I can name them for you here in disposition of power.

Harley. Could I have chosen a better name myself? He was the shortest of them but easily the most vicious, but probably not the most dangerous, at least in close quarters. I am hard pressed to say that this is a necessary trait of a leader, but I would listen to any argument supporting the theory. He was nearly as wide as he was tall, not fat, but built like a front-loading washing machine and, as with such a machine, it was easy to see that things were turning within, though one would be challenged to identify any one article of clothing, save for perhaps a shoe. Unlike the bleached white smocks and slacks of his comrades, he was clad in powder blue, a distinction that quite discernibly pleased him. He, at times, could appear almost handsome, or at least not ugly, no doubt a function of his functional, if only utilitarian, intelligence. His head was square, in thematic concert with his body. His hair was receded and regrettably long in the back. He had meeting eyebrows, not so much almond as Brazil-nut-shaped eyes, large and round and close-to-his-head ears, a large convex nose with turned-down nostrils, a short mouth with straight lips, a square and jutting chin, and no facial hair to speak of. I suppose the same is true of all of us, that a mere catalog of our physiognomy sounds rather unprepossessing and repulsive, but somehow all of his features were worn in the right places and in more-or-less standard proportion and so the overall effect was not too terribly bad. He walked with a slight but conspicuous limp; the favored side seemed to change periodically, leaving Billy to conclude that his shoes were too tight and hurt his feet and that particular pairs caused diversely distributed pain. I admonished Billy about his tasteless alliteration but had to concur. Harley was complex enough that the mere acquisition of the property of others was not the sole motivating principle behind his odious behavior, though it was in no way insignificant. It was the power dynamic within his herd that drove him and I believed that it was finally sexual, that lording over his subordinates actually gave him a boner. What came of that erection, and for that phrasing I apologize, I did not know and I did not care to imagine. Harley was also fond of a particular cologne, the name of which I did not know, and it was either extremely potent or he bathed in it.

Tommy was a beanpole with two left feet. Literally, he had two left feet. When he faced north both of his big toes pointed east. It turns out that it is true what they say about the clumsiness of dancers so endowed. Merely walking was a challenge and made for a sideways, crablike gait that was both noisy and profoundly ugly. I believed that his constant shuffling and stumbling kept him in his nasty, contemptible mood. On his most pleasant days he was dismissive and scornful. On his worst he was hateful, black hearted, and monstrous, rolling over slippered toes with wheelchairs that he was shoving at life-threatening speeds through congested hallways. It may well be that there was not an honest bone in his sinister, left-leaning body and I never once heard him say anything that was factual, even in response to the most mundane and seemingly simple questions, even when the facts were unmissable, staring him and whomever else in the face. When asked by a day nurse if Abraham Chen's prosthetic leg had been left back in his rooms, he responded, No, I put it on him before we left, leaving the nurse and Abraham Chen to exchange confounded glances. But I'll take him back so that I can tighten the strap, Tommy then said. If such a thing was possible, I was of the opinion that the man had two left eyes as well, a condition that manifested in a barely perceptible but constant pull of his face to that direction. There was a rumor that Tommy liked to sneak sly ganders at the old ladies when they were being bathed or taken to the bathroom. Though I never (Allah be praised) saw him doing so, it was easy enough, however sickening and repulsive the picture, to imagine his depraved and salacious, distorted, left-eyed squint around this corner or that.

Cletus. Cletus was a troll of a man, Nordic in appearance, with a patch covering, I think, his good eye, and he possessed upper incisors that presented like tusks. His hair in troll fashion was thick and uncombable and Billy thought on more than one occasion that a tail was hidden in his white britches. He wore a gold cross on a cheap gold chain around his neck, no doubt the source of his power. He had lived near humans long enough to have learned many of our ways and so he was conscientious about pleasant greetings but always managed to make us regret it in short order. Though not as short as Harley, he was far slighter, weighing perhaps as much as a woman of equal height, his protruding ears like wings. If he had not been so repugnant in appearance, he might not have been frightening at all, but there was a sneakiness about him that one could almost smell. It wasn't that it seemed he wanted something, but it seemed he was going to take something. Though none of us carried wallets or purses, we clung to them anyway in his presence. He smelled vaguely sweet but not good. Whenever he skipped down the corridor, and he often did, I could hear Grieg's *In the Hall of the Mountain King.* Now, I knew that trolls are not naturally evil, only misunderstood and, of course, primitive, but he was, if not evil, then he might as well have been evil.

Leon was truly the brute of the lot. At over six and a half feet, he lumbered about like the giant he was, broadshouldered, deep-chested, stronglimbed, and brawnyhanded; his ridiculously large feet, hard like hooves in the most padded of gym shoes, announced his approach in oddly syncopated *whumps* upon the linoleum tiles. He always sounded as if he'd just stopped and then another footfall would shake the floor. Whether he was Fafner or Fasolt, it didn't matter; he could have been both, but he would never have been lithe enough to catch Freyja. He was ungainly beyond reasonable belief; so inelegant was he in movement that Harley would not allow him to be in the same space as Tommy and his two left feet, perhaps for consideration of safety, more, I like to think, for aesthetic reasons. Leon's hands were too large for many common tasks, though he was strangely adept at threading needles, which I saw him do twice. Once for Regina Brown, who was working on an embroidery, and then for a temporary night nurse upon whom he held an obvious crush and with whom he held not even the slightest chance. His head was shaved, but he was lazy and so his head was only nearly smooth, but not smooth enough to appear clean, plant matter and lint and dust seeming to find its static charge irresistible. Six cubits and a span in height, Billy would say of the man, referring to biblical Goliath. I used to be a religious man, a real scripture reader, he said, and then my balls were excised by German shrapnel. My faith went with them. Leon, like Tommy, could sneak up on no one. In fact, none of the already-mentioned thugs had stealth as a weapon, Harley being always announced by his fragrance and Cletus being subject to involuntary fits of giggling.

Ramona. The only woman among the terrible tribe, but one would hardly have known it. Stealth was in fact her first and most striking power. She was a creeper, having the annoying habit of materializing at one's shoulder out of the crystalline blue. Ramona was of medium height and build and of a bit less than medium intelligence. It seemed that she ran with the boys because they were the only game in town, so to speak. In some raggedy village on the steppes of Uzbekistan or Kyrgyzstan or Turkmenistan, she might have been considered mildly appealing, what with her exaggerated but not so well-defined biceps and broad back. The K-Swiss gym shoes she wore were always impossibly white and unblemished, even after bouts of mopping up diarrhea, blood, or vomit. She wore a ring on the fourth finger of her left hand, though I did not believe her to be married or even attached to another living human animal. When she spoke it was always a loud whisper, a deafening hiss that went unmissed by anyone within a range of thirty or more feet. Ramona spoke in apparent non sequiturs, but her utterances were actually always just a few minutes behind everyone else, if not her actions. Tommy and Cletus were once trying to get an administrative office door unstuck, having just come in from their smoking break with Ramona. Ramona watched for a few seconds and when asked for a flat-head screwdriver from the box, she said, I don't have any cigarettes, but she passed along the tool without pause. The oddest thing was that from her cavernous mouth, a mouth that remained slightly open for breathing, came the warmest breath, breath one was prepared to find foul but it was not, yet neither did it smell good. It was merely warm.

Finally there was the unfortunately named **Billy.** The old Billy did call him Silly but also referred to him as Billy Dud, a more appropriate nickname, as Silly almost made him sound interesting. Billy

Dud was so frightfully bland that mosquitoes refused to stick their proboscises into him, treated him as if he'd been soaked in DEET. He was pure, unadulterated background, complete camouflage, a sort of ninja of boredom. If he leaned against a wall, he became the wall. If he carried large cartons, he became a carton. His voice was white noise. He was a chameleon, fading, receding, into the back of any room as if on greased rails, smoothly, effortlessly, a complete forgettable slide to some corner or other. He was a member of the wicked crew only by passive attachment. It was not clear that the others were even aware of his membership or him. They probably wondered on occasion while smoking in the courtyard, just to whom did that sixth shadow belong? The strangest thing about Billy Dud was that once you did catch a glimpse of him you realized that he was beautiful, damn beautiful. But then he would open his mouth and then the mind-numbing, characterless, vanilla static would wash over you and the room and you would be left wondering what you had seen.

If you live long enough you come to understand that the only terrifying thing is not knowing when a thing is going to happen, whether good or bad. And the older you get, the more you count on knowing when things are going to happen. Bad things, uncomfortable things, death things, are only unsettling and dismaying when they fail to comply with the schedule, the scheme, the plan. The scariest thing about the Gang of Six, as Billy had dubbed them, was that they had no obvious schedule and no apparent goals. One evening, after dinner, after Billy Dud had blended into the salad bar of the dining hall, Harley came in to check the pockets of everyone for suspected illicit drugs. The only staff there were the orderlies, the food workers having been escorted out by the giant Leon. Many of the residents, especially the blue-haired old women at the next table, always accused old Billy of being paranoid and therefore a nuisance, but tonight all were on the same dismal page of shared humiliation. The Gang laughed when a condom was found in Sheldon Cohen's pocket. Cohen had been a medical doctor and I did not know if he was having sex with anyone, but he wanted at least to be safe and prepared if the opportunity and other things arose. I never saw a man over seventy so embarrassed; it's really not something we feel. Finding no banned substances, the goons left with whatever cash they could find. Billy stood and shouted out his displeasure. Do you hooligans know no shame!

Even I had to admit that his word choice was antiquated and therefore undercutting of any gravity he hoped to convey.

Hooligans? Harley smiled and stepped up face to neck with Billy. Sit down, old man.

I will report you.

Go ahead. Tell them what the big bad hooligans did. He looked around the room, Just remember, all of you, that it will be weeks before any action is taken. Weeks. With that he pressed his meaty palm into Billy's chest and forced him back down into his chair.

Had you followed Billy back to his apartment after the above-described confrontation with Harley that took place at the end of the insane ratification of his rants against the Gang, you would have seen him open that briefcase that he kept stowed on the bottom shelf of his bookcase and take out hand-drawn maps of the community complex and grounds that he had composed and amended over his ten-year residency at Teufelsdröckh. Then, as he placed himself over the spread-out papers, you would have seen him scratching crazily at the back of his head and pulling on his thumbs the way he always did when excited or nervous. But it was not specifically this night that had Billy pondering over his charts. He did so every night, his pencil making slight and subtle altera-tions to tables and diagrams and even graphs, tracking the com-ings and leavings of the Gang members, their combinations, what they were carrying. Billy never seemed to know just what he was looking for, but that night, he pointed at me with end of his num-ber two pencil. It's up to you, he said.

What's up to me?

You have to sneak into the break room and take Cletus's keys.

Excuse me?

I would do it, but I'm old.

I'm seventy-eight.

I'm glad we're on the same page. This is how it has to go.

The summer evening had begun to fold the world in its myste-rious embrace. Except that the sun had set hours ago and no rest was to come to my storm-tossed heart. I was to put on my darkest clothes and time it all *just right*.

12

The orderlies' break room was set at the southeast corner of the central building on campus, a square, characterless block of pale-red bricks that housed the dining facilities and the administrative offices, such as they were. That the break room was on that particular corner was hardly of any consequence, since I had no sense of directional orientation, but to Billy it was the linchpin of the entire operation. He reasoned that as I was setting out at dusk the fact that that side of the building would be darker would be to my advantage. In fact, it did not matter at all, and I didn't point it out to him that the whole perimeter of the building was fairly well lit. What was useful were Billy's markings of the security guard's nightly rounds, of which there was essentially one. At six, upon arriving for his shift, he would make a leisurely circle about the building and then settle in behind his desk at the front door and watch blue movies on his player under the counter. He thought he was being covert in his activity, but he was hard of hearing and so the sound was turned up just loud enough that even we, those with a bit of deafness, could hear the moaning. I imagined the movies to not be hard-core, as they said, but rather the kinds of movies I had see advertised in my town newspaper when I was a kid, the ads saying to call the theater for the title. Billy and I had agreed, read Billy had explained, that entry into the break room was to be best achieved through the window on the south wall that seemed to always be open and also offered the cover of some star jasmine bushes. That was reasonable enough. My mission, my assignment, was to collect as many keys as I could find, we would figure out to which locks the keys matched and how to best use them later, and to bury them behind the azaleas outside my apartment. My heart was racing as I leaned against that exterior wall, not so much out of fear but because I had just performed my version of a sprint across the hundred-yard lawn. The sprinklers came on just as I slapped my back against the bricks, either luck or bad timing because I had told Billy that I could make the run in a third the time. A look into the room confirmed that it was empty and the sound of the sprinklers covered my prying of the screen loose from the window. The plan was working beautifully. However, there is nothing quite so inelegant as an old man climbing through a window. A thousand sprinklers could not have masked the noise I made knocking over a table with a hot plate and plastic dishes and a chair on which had sat a large metal mixing bowl that now served as a bouncing gong. Luckily the guard could not hear it or was otherwise engaged, an image I tried to instantly expel. At any rate, I stood there, frozen, wondering why I would choose to freeze in plain view instead of hastily trying to hide or to crawl right back out the window through which I had just come. But I paused there for many seconds, as much to let my back ease into uprightness as anything else, until I was satisfied that no one was coming. I put back the table and chair and bowl and then I searched surfaces, lockers, and pockets and found a ring with eight keys, seven rather conventional and one old skeleton type. I was just about to exit when I heard movement in the corridor. I ducked into a corner beside the row of lockers and behind a chair draped with an orderly's white uniform.

13

The first thing I thought of as I crouched there trying to control my breathing was something my father once said to me. Never trust anyone who has not read *An Occurrence at Owl Creek Bridge*. He said it to me one night at dinner. He pointed his fork at me while he said it. I heard someone grip and begin to turn the doorknob. I thought about proper names, specifically the question of whether proper names have senses, a question I came to again and again. Can *your father = your grandfather's son,* if true (if I can let these descriptions stand in for proper names, be names of names), differ in analytical value from *your father = your father? Your father* and *your grandfather's son* have the same reference but perhaps possess different senses.

I recalled when I was adult, it was 1965 and in the paper was one of those ads for a movie that required a telephone call to the theater to learn the title. Just like when I was a preteen, though we weren't preteens back then but squirts and punks, I called the theater and was told that the title of the film was *High Yellow*. So, I went to it and it turned out to be pretty much the same as that Louise Beavers and Claudette Colbert film *Imitation of Life*. It could have been called *Imitation of Imitation of Life*. Even though I was an adult by this time, I had still come to a movie the title of which I had obtained by calling the theater, and so I waited and waited for the blue part, the sex. It never came. I think some skinny white guy who got kicked out of West Point for maybe being gay kissed the light-skinned black girl who was passing for white and perhaps that was the blue part, the scandalous part, but I didn't know and I didn't care. I returned home that night and tried to save myself by reading Tully. Was that the same as reading Cicero?

I recalled Plutarch's account of Cicero's death. Apparently he was difficult to find until Antony's soldiers caught him leaving his villa in a litter. How hard would it be to find a man in a litter carried by slaves? From his own villa? According to Dio, not known for his accuracy, Antony's wife ripped out the tongue of the already-detached-and-nailed-to-the-Forum-wall head of Tully and poked it repeatedly with a needle or some other ignominious sharp instrument. Empires. Civilization.

And then I thought about *An Occurrence at Owl Creek Bridge* and remembered that on the end of my father's fork was a bit of linguiça.

14

Balled up there as I was, time having sadistically stood still to allow the locking of my ankles, knees, and back, I was not prepared to have my heart somewhat broken. The nurse who every day dispensed my Losartan, Cissy, whose name I found as intriguing as her short-cut afro, walked into the room with Harley. There was an unadorned cot in the break room and to my dismay, mainly out of disdain for cliché, they sat on it. Cissy kicked off her white clogs and thank goodness for those clunky shoes as it was her footfalls that alerted me to their approach. Her beige feet were beautiful and they wore jeweled toe rings and beside her sat that camel Harley. He reached back to the switch on the wall and killed the light, mercifully sparing me the actual sight of young Cissy so compromised. Now, the only light was outside and around that square portal that was my way out. I could hear them and therefore all too well imagine the progress of their activity and I was reminded for some inexplicable reason of the mandibles of grasshoppers. This was some motivation to make a snappy exit, but more pressing was the pressure that I was experiencing in my lower abdomen. A quick and undesired glance at the huffing animals showed me Harley's hairy back and Cissy's bejeweled toes pointed toward the sprinklers on the ceiling. The cot was rickety and squeaky and Harley was an unselfconscious, grunting swine and so I made as little noise as possible as I set the metal bowl on the floor and used the chair to climb up and back through the window. I could not help but cast one more glance back at the cot and when I did I saw that Cissy was observing me. She offered a small smile and almost nodded and for the briefest second I imagined that she had come there to help me, but I knew that couldn't be so. I found myself smiling, glancing askance at her mocking eye, but she was not mocking me but nodding or nearly nodding her complicity in my escape. I knew it couldn't be so. The smelly beast was inside her and she closed her eyes and let her head fall back. The odor of their sex was like burnt flesh and the dung of storks and flamingos and mouthfuls of tea. I wanted her to hate it. I wanted him to be a pathetic lover. I wanted Cissy to suddenly push him off and away and say that she had come to her senses and was going home. Instead, she moaned. And I believed her.

Good idea that, the getting away. It was quite dark out now save for where I was standing, bathed in a spotlight between two jasmine bushes. The heady fragrance of the little white flowers was welcome as it served to wash the insides of my nostrils clean of the stench of that horrid and unholy sex. I found myself blinded momentarily by the flood lamp and then I started my sprint back across the lawn. Mind you, I could have been timed with a calendar, but I moved as fast as I could and no one saw me and no one saw as I used the trowel I had left behind the azaleas below my window to dig a hole for the keys.

15

The keys were in the hole behind the azaleas and I sat sweaty in a fake leather recliner in Billy's bedroom while he laid out a set of nice clothes, dress clothes, a gray suit with vest, a red tie with a thin gray stripe down its center length, a crisp white shirt with French cuffs, cuff links, and tie clasp set neatly on the tie, black socks that had never been worn. He did this every night and every night the outfit was slightly different, he believing and stating that every day he was a different man and the day he awoke to find that that was not true would be the day he was dead and these clothes that he had laid out would be his coffin garb, his funeral wear, because he didn't trust anyone else to pick out what he would be cremated in, yes, cremated, he said, You don't bury a man with no balls and that hole-in-the-ground thing reminded him too much of foxholes in the war anyway, reminded him of the particular foxhole where he had left a favorite part of himself. This tie was a gift from my daughter. It is a terrible, terrible thing to outlive your child.

Yes, I know.

The Chinese call it the curse of the gods.

I know.

I was never the same again. I've lived two lifetimes longer than my beloved child.

16

No metaphor ever replaced thought or so was my judgment until a metaphor did become thought for me, the metaphor not only replaced thought but organically pushed thought back to the most basic and functional areas of life and existence. The metaphor did not derive out of an extension of some thought and so relied on nothing really for actuality, substance, or even tenor, but appeared, arrived complete, like one of Leibniz's monads and like a universe unto itself the metaphor was forever collapsing in on itself while giving the appearance of expansion, a good trick if you don't mind cleaning up a mess. When I was a kid I realized that if I chopped off all of my fingers, I'd still have hands, not very good hands, not quite functional hands, but hands. What happened to your hands? some insensitive and pathologically honest child would ask me. A lot, I would say. And if I chopped off both hands to my wrists, they would still ask, What happened to your hands? but mean something else.

How farther art this in headland, hellhole, be the same. Die keen drum dumb, die kill beat drum, dawn dearth ass with ill den even. Rive dust gist weigh dour gaily dead, sand relieve just tour dress patches, alas we relieve clothes due dress patch relent gust, kin leave rust snot unto our nation, cut shiver lust from Melville. Core dine in this thief dome and the sour and the gory, endeavor, endeavor. End it how you like.

I was never much with prayers, but all superstitions have their place.

17

My wife did not fall in love with me because of it, but she did turn
my way when I noted that she was wearing a Watteau. It was red
satin and she looked nice.

What's a Watteau?

A French Rococo-era painter. And a style of formal dress, popular in the early eighteenth century.

And she was dressed this way because?

It was a costume ball, some museum event or other. Sometimes
you'll see a Watteau train on a wedding dress these days. It's pleated
down the back.

And how were you dressed for this ball?

I went as Nat Turner.

How did you know what a Watteau was?

My education, I guess. The irony of Nat Turner recognizing a
Watteau was not lost on her.

I've never been to a costume party.

How do you know?

You should tell stories from now on without my interruptions.

The way *you* tell stories.

The way *I* tell stories.

18

The Gang of Six strode into our building chanting, but not in unison and so it made for loathsome and hard-featured music. The gist of their rant-chanting was that we were in trouble, all of us and of course we knew they were coming, as all the custodians had disappeared and as well as the night nurse. *Keys* seemed to be the key word in their chorus. All the residents shrank away and gave sidelong glances that made every one of them look as guilty as hell. All except Billy, who barked into the air, not directly at them, If you can't keep up with your toys, maybe you shouldn't have them. Billy did in fact have balls. I stood firm. Though frightening, they could not match so much that I had seen in life. I noticed a bit of dirt under one of my nails and shoved my hands in my pockets.

> *Memetne adloqueris?*
> *Sprichst du mit mir?*
> *Tu me parles?*
> *Du taler til mig?*
> *Stai parlando con me?*

By some dissymmetry, the underlying reasons of which elude me, however much constructed, affirmed, and validated by the very structure of the language that allows at least a pretense of making meaning, I am able to reveal my story without locating myself in the telling, at the time of the telling. Perhaps not even whether I am in fact the narrator at all. It would appear, at least on the surface, that I am necessarily, logically committed to choosing either past, present, or future tense for my narration, but I will demonstrate that was not true. There is nothing instantaneous in these or in any pages you will ever read. If it is written down, it was written down, it is dated and it turns out that measurement is neither important nor possible. For example, this sentence was or is being written one year and a day after the composition of the preceding sentence. I am lying. I wrote the second sentence first, two days prior to the first, or was it two minutes? at the same time, one with my left hand, the other with my right.

Harley winked. His eyes twinkled. All right, all right, forget all you know. This is a new day. Come out of your fog, old people. Adopt this new day. Give me my keys and the storm will be but a drizzle. If we search and find the keys in your possession, there will be hell to pay.

There was no talking among us old people. We were being inconvenienced. We were not terrified. Not one of us had had a normal bowel movement in years. We kept track of wellness by measurements and marked the progress of days by counted-out pills. We had seen death. We had buried children. They could not scare us. All we had left was our dignity.

Only Billy and I knew the whereabouts of the keys and no one would find them. The thugs sought more to make messes than to perform thorough searches and so they did. We old people did not care. Cleaning up gave us something to do. They concluded with Billy's apartment. The brute Leon and Harley entered shoulder to elbow and we listened from the corridor.

Cletus and Ramona blocked the door. I stood with Billy, held his hand. I looked at Cletus's head. It was a strange-looking machine with a huge set of gears that did not mesh, connecting with a series of drumlike rollers. I turned to Ramona and observed on her shoulder a small woman, dressed like her host and using a shovel to scoop up brown crystals from a pile in the hollow of Ramona's clavicle and pitch them into Ramona's dumbstruck open mouth.

Ed ella a me: Nessun maggior dolore,
Che ricordarsi del tempo felice
Nella miseria; e ciò sa 'l tuo dottore.

A crash of glass. Glass crash. Crash. Billy and I knew. The fuse had been lit and Billy let go of my hand. On the wall of his living room had hung a framed photograph of Billy as a much younger man and his daughter. She was twenty-five at the time of its taking. A year later she would be gone. It was one of those color portraits that you hate unless you love the people in it. She was positioned just behind her father, just over his left shoulder. She stood. Billy sat. Her hands were on him, her left on his left shoulder, her right gently, just barely, touching the right side of his collar and neck. Together they stared at the camera but somehow gave the impression of staring at each other, as if looking into a mirror. Billy's hands were not in the photograph, but I felt the tension of his wanting to reach up and touch his daughter's fingers, her face. It was that framed picture that had crashed to the floor. Billy shouted something I could not make out but understood all too well and then started toward the door of his apartment faster than his ninety-year-old legs were capable of moving. He fell, not in slow motion, but quickly, and that was the real horror of the sight, a man who always shifted so slowly through his range of positions was now moving rapidly. I think his head hit the baseboard, but whatever, all became immediately still, especially Billy.

19

An old man, with his beautiful daughter on his arm, walks through a park, along a street, emerges from the smoke of a dream and into some light that falls from a shop's window. Behind the window, laid on a black fabric, are beads of gold and silver. Seated inside, sidelong to the window, is an old man, his face bent earnestly over the open workings of a watch. I gazed with little or no interest at the gears and springs.

I am not a man of science. I am not proficient in any branch of nature study. I do not know the difference between an amphibian and a reptile. I have no yearning for hard knowledge about the hard world. And yet I have no affinity for anything spiritual. In fact, I have a pronounced, conspicuous, and striking absence of an affinity for anything spiritual.

I know but one hard thing about the hard world and it is this: from the sum of all theories, as arranged in accordance with ascertained facts, we make a few assumptions, that we have actually ascertained facts, that we are actually here to ascertain them, and that there is actually a *here.*

20

So you are a writer, Billy had once said to me as we sat at the picnic table on the lawn.

Apparently.

How come I've never heard of you?

Your poor education?

He laughed.

I'll bet my daughter knew your work. She was a real reader. And not that romance stuff or just detective books. Real stuff like Goethe and Joyce.

That's wonderful.

What kinds of things did you write?

His use of the past tense bothered me, but at our ages everything seemed to be in the past tense. I wrote some novels.

If I could see worth a damn I'd ask to read one of them.

Thank you, Billy.

I was just a simple accountant.

I nodded. I had heard this before and the punch line that would follow.

Everybody likes an accountant with no balls. Not your tax man, you want your tax man to have balls, but not your accountant. He looked at his thumbnail, slowly raised it to his mouth and tried to bite it. My daughter was an angel. She had knock knees.

You don't see too many girls with those anymore.

Do you have a middle name?

I do. And you?

It's Virgil.

21

Thanks ever so much for the footnote, said he,
Thanks ever so much for the plug.
Thanks for the roses and very strong tea,
And for business swept under the rug.

Remember the pudding we dined on last night,
The wine and that stinky bit of cheese,
And jot down the names of those still all right
And tuck them away with the keys.

Dream of a place under the evening star
And of pigeons all lined in a row,
Of asphodels, lilies, and blooms without scent
And the tugging of the undertow.

Recall the pudding we dined on last night,
The wine and rather rank cheese.
Jot down the names to be read in the light
And tuck them away with the keys, the keys,
Tuck them away with keys.

22

When you kick out for yourself, my dear, and you will, remember, whatever you do, to find good people to be your friends. Billy had regained consciousness but not his complete senses. I was both his daughter and myself, it seemed. He was in a bed in a room in the hospital building of Teufelsdröckh. He then said, You know, we are as old as we feel.

How old do you feel, my friend?

I am a mountain.

I asked the doctor, a man not as old as a plumber's new watch, how Billy was doing.

He's ninety, the doctor said.

Immediately I had renewed respect for his judgment and his profession. I nodded.

Always build one door opposite another so that birds, bats, and the wind have a way out. It will also allow your house to become a flute, if it so chooses.

23

Were I to begin this all again, here and undeferred and non-circuitously, I might begin: The river runs past Eden, from the sag of the shore to the bend of the bay, delivering us back to where we first set about. But I cannot begin this all again and, what is more, I would not, will not, shall not. Never keep all of your allusions in one basket. And never assume there is not a fish at the end of your line.

Why are you talking like that?

I thought you were asleep.

How can I sleep with you spouting that gibberish and with all these hellish machines beeping and screaming every few seconds?

Are you feeling stronger?

Billy ignored the question. Tell them they don't need these machines. I'll let them know when I'm dead. Or you'll let them know. They might not trust you at first, but they'll finally believe you. He lay back and closed his eyes. Have you ever contemplated the meaning of life?

The meaning of life is the purpose of life. I'd settle for any meaning at all.

Is it going to rain?

The photograph is fine, a little wrinkled, but fine.

Billy nodded. Give them hell. Say something else crazy, like you were saying before.

I don't have any more gibberish.

Of course you do. You're full of it.

Once upon a time, Billy, once upon a time.

He spoke with his eyes shut, his lids fluttering. I don't believe in god and so I don't believe in heaven, but still I hope to see my little girl's face.

I know just what you mean.

Come now, just a wee bit more from the fountain of nonsense?

Come forth, Lazarus! And he came fifth and lost his job.

I knew you had it in you.

And so Billy ceased breathing and stopped his blood from circulating, though I believe his brain was still doing brain things. His unsympathetic, attendant machines announced his resolution in concert monotone. The doctor and a nurse clogged into the room to stand motionless at the foot of the bed. He's gone, I said, and to my surprise they believed me.

*N*o Living Word

24

Once upon the middle of a story—in the remote distance dense plumes of smoke mingled with jets of flame that gushed forth from an immense pile of earthly dividers—the multitude of common spectators sent up an ecstatic shout and clapped hands with an emphasis that made the welkin echo. Throughout that room there was the same obscurity as before, but not the same gloom associated with Billy's loss. No flame had vanished and the whole scene remained.

That night I brought in the keys from the hole behind the azaleas beneath my window, removed them from the plastic bag from the Rite Aid pharmacy, and sorted them by size, then color. Keys. Blades and bows. I again paused at the very old-looking one, so primitive and so strange.

25

Murky as it is, the conventional precept that the idea *signification* contains an augmentation/intensification uncertainty has rather obvious ramifications. The theory that the signification of a term is, in fact, a concept supports the implication that significations actually have individual substance. But are not the significations here for all of us? Are they not public? I'm afrege this is true. Maybe not. Cannot the same be signified for more than one person regardless of psychological predisposition or disposition, for that matter? Even still, understanding the signification, grasping the individual substance of such a thing, is an act of cognitive individuation. So then it comes down to the occupation of a particular and singular, if not nameable or isolatable, psychological state for some meaning to be available or even possible. Alcohol.

This I thought while dead Billy sat at my table. We were drinking. I more than he. He was contained in a forest-green cremation urn wrapped with three tan stripes and a tan cap. It was shaped a like Russian nesting doll and maybe it was, because I never opened it. I would scatter you someplace, my friend, but I would not know where.

Thankfully, Billy did not reply.

We went through the keys together. Some were obviously door keys, others keys to either cabinets or locks. A couple were certainly padlock keys. None was marked in any way to yield to me its corresponding lock. Billy suggested that I take one short key and one long, or at least two keys quite dissimilarly shaped, and search with them alone until I discovered their mates in the world. This made sense. I would not confuse the keys and I could finally create a key to the keys. And then I would devise a plan for my keys.

And what is this one?

Odd, isn't it?

Billy held the old rusty key and studied it. It must be a keepsake or a charm. It certainly opens no door around here.

Like Zeno to the roost, you are. When was the last time you visited? I know, I know, you just can't seem to get here or there or anywhere for that matter. Half a step, half a step, half a step home. There is a nice nurse at the desk during the afternoon into the evening. I like her short hair because it does not make her look like a boy. I like her in spite of her taste in men. But because of her taste in men, I can know a little. A little about whens and wheres, goings and comings. And she keeps my secret, our secret, and so I guess that makes us accomplices and I guess that means we're on the same side and I suppose that means we share the same enemies and I wonder if that means that I am all wrong about her taste in men.

26

Dear Adverbs, Adverbial Phrases, and Turns of Phrase,

I am writing to express, an odious word, perhaps rather then, to impress upon you, in no uncertain terms, enthusiastically even, my indebtedness to you. Your unqualified and qualifying force, your abating timbre, your mitigating music, your bombastic possibility, oh, how gently you insert yourselves, allowing such modest station as extraneous expression, superfluous excess. I will *probably, without a doubt,* and *without fail* admit to your undying, if I may be so dramatic, importance to the language I speak, and you would do well to recognize that the language to which I refer is not English, but, merely, crucially, human language. It has taken me, and I hate even to count, many years to so happily employ my unused and, surprisingly, up until recently, unwanted and, largely, unnoticed supply of *ly*'s.

Yours ever so truly,

I have been reduced to addressing parts of speech, as if they might answer and of course they do. I was thinking I might chat up nouns next when the short, copper-colored key with the rubber head cover opened the drug locker on the west building nurse's station. I slipped the key into my pocket just as the nurse rounded the corner. It was in fact the nurse who had seen me in the orderlies' break room. She gave me a suspicious look. I had seen her name tag many times, had known her name, yet this time the pin that adorned her breast spoke to me. Delilah.

Delilah Zorn was around twenty-five years old and beautiful, and as an old man, I can say this, having seen many, many people in my long life. She was graceful, light on her feet, though I would not say she floated, and her skin was a rich reddish brown that seemed to glow yet did not. She was too beautiful to imagine with

Harley, so I chose not to, choice being an important activity that I seldom employed in my first sixty years of life. Choice is more complicated than it first seems. There is the axiom of choice that makes me happy just to consider but confuses me when I do, the notion that for every collection of nonempty sets there is a function that chooses an element from each set. I assume that we are each, at least, a nonempty set, even any of the Gang of Six, even Hitler, Cheney, or some other war criminal. So, I made such a choice and Delilah Zorn remained a flower, a star, a waterfall, a stand of aspens.

What were you doing back there, she said.

I learned long ago that the worst answer to any question is nothing, the word or no response. I said, I have a headache and was looking for something to take.

What kind of headache?

Sinus.

Here, take these.

Do you like working at this place? I asked. I had closed my hand around the two pills she had given me.

It pays the bills, she said.

Thank you for the medicine.

Why were you in there? she asked.

Why didn't you give me away?

I'm not sure.

Do you like that man, that Harley?

Not particularly. Her answer seemed to surprise both of us. I didn't tell him because I hate to see trouble.

I was looking for something.

I figured that much. What?

Something they took from Billy.

What is it? Maybe I can help.

I found it. But thank you.

It wasn't keys.

No.

Do you have any children? she asked.

My son was born probably thirty years before you. You see, I'm
a very old man.

Not so old, she said. You still have a twinkle in your eye.

Cataracts.

We were flirting. A sad activity. A bit of push. A bit of pull.

Der ganze Strudel strebt nach oben:

Du glaubst zu schieben, und du wirst geschoben.

27

I have a second face.

Perhaps a third.

Access to separate worlds.

The awful and the fruit litter my worlds at the same time. Oh, January, dear Janus, Ianus Bifrons, guardian of doors and gates, looking both forward and back. Up past the pines someplace, past the aspens, is Zoagli, with its view of the sea. Behold the sign.

In a dream, in the repetition of the dream, the riddle is solved. I kill myself as my father in order to commit incest with myself as my mother, but as my father I prevent my own conception.

Leben wir oder werden wir gelebt?

28

Sheldon Cohen had been a doctor and he was proud that, unlike so many in his profession, he had lived well into his nineties. He also boasted an every-morning gotta-pee erection that I was privileged never to witness, but he talked about it unabashedly with anyone who would listen. Ninety-four with a boner, he would say at the breakfast table full of old ladies. He never mentioned it at lunch or dinner, I assumed because he had forgotten about it by then, but the ladies didn't forget and so raced to his table at every meal. Since Billy's death Sheldon had taken to sitting with me and therefore so did five women.

Who's to say they won't kill one of us next, said Maria Cortez. She was always dressed impeccably. She was still beautiful even though she was hunched over a bit. She knew she was beautiful and moved in that way. Billy was kind.

Billy was a sour cherry pit, said Mrs. Klink. I believe her first name was Mrs. I took to calling her Mrs. and she never objected. She was always extremely direct, even when she was flirting with an episode of dementia, as when she said to me at lunch, You've mown the grass horribly, Philbert. You've missed all the edges. You are a wretched man. All I could focus on was the fact that her husband's name was Philbert Klink. I imagined him unhappy. But that's not the point, she went on. They will kill all of us and rummage through our things.

We're old people, Emily Kuratowski said. She was a small woman with piercing eyes that never seemed to point anywhere. What can they do to us that will really matter? We're nearly dead anyway.

Hear, hear, said Mrs. Klink.

Billy did not die happily or happy, I said. They turned and stared at me because I was generally the quiet one of the newly formed group. We can make sure they don't win. We can get even for Billy.

Yeah, right, said Emily Kuratowski. What will that do for us?

It might satisfy us.

We're long past satisfaction, Maria said.

Okay, then it might amuse us.

The group paused at the word. They liked the idea of being entertained. Their old heads nodded, then nodded some more.

I'd like to be amused, Sheldon said. Lord knows I'm not getting any action around here.

Maria Cortez gave Sheldon's arm a playful slap. Stop it, you.

What do we do? Mrs. Klink asked.

They all looked to me. I had already, fueled by an new and inconsonant desire for revenge and an even more uncharacteristic willingness to take action, decided to take the lead. Though I had no plan, I understood that our objectives would have to be clear, simple, and quick and without too much ambition, as my comrades were subject to sudden slips into other worlds and times and, for all I knew, so was I.

29

In my rooms I stood and studied my little kitchen area and was re-minded of Cornell's *Toward the Blue Peninsula,* imagining the steps from my little range to my little icebox, then marveled at how my use of the term *icebox* dated me so efficiently, so uncomplicatedly. It might be easier, I thought, it might be easier.

I sat in my living room without lamplight and pulled out a ran-dom book from my pile—a pile that throughout my life was con-stantly growing but was now steadily diminishing, my being well past mezzo del cammin di nostra vita—Dante's *Inferno.* I opened it but did not read. I cried. About Billy. About your mother. About you. And it was not ugly music. Io non piangeva, si dentro impie-trito. Forever the pounder of metaphor, the seeker of stretched con-nection, the pioneer of extended conjunction, I imagined the Gang or orderlies as the six wings of Lucifer, beating to free him from the ice and creating an icy wind that only creates more ice.

And so you've come to visit and you've written your visit into actuality or I have written this for you, once again, though none it matters a hill of whatever now, does it? You asked me once if I was postmodern and I asked you if your question contained a hy-phen. I finally have an answer and I offer it here as it is apropos of my following dear Virgil down Satan's shivering, hairy back. I finally have figured out I do not wish to deny being a modernist by trying to embrace all that is familiar while pretending to not be concerned with making something brand spanking new. I do not wish to create new clichés. But neither will I bare my soul to build the new machine that no one has seen just to have it do what the old machine did. So, what am I about, son? Dying, son. Dying well. Dying powerfully, vigorously, with might and main, to chop and change to suit my dying mission, to tie dying ever to life, to living, to breathing, to tie dying to the moon and the stars, to fix dying to light and darkness and rain and mist and arid winds.

Preface

I don't know if readers will like your novel, if you choose to write your novel or take credit, perhaps blame, for having written your novel, I don't know, just don't know if they will like the turns it takes, the turns you find so pleasing, its comedy, its fantastic elements, the pones you consider passably original, its relaxed and natural transition, except where abrupt and intentionally jarring, the curious, unconventional mixture of different styles that gives the work a distinctive air, leaving you to hope that you entertain, perhaps upset, maybe frighten a reader . . . but what a bad preface I have written for you, leaving you nothing to do but tenaciously cling to your conclusions; this is a funny book with natural transitions, except where abrupt, with original fantastical elements; and if all that is true, then your work is beautiful; says who? How bizarre a reader you construct, because you do construct her, him, it, don't you? How bizarre that reader must be to ingest your preface and believe it or at least not abandon your projected desires concerning your so-called novel. However, in fact, your book might seem to begin in the manner of a definition dialogue, setting out to identify rhetorical stratagems, but concludes, as perhaps all things conclude, appearing as little more than an attempt to discern how one can best find some happiness in this life. Whereas we might be moved to plausibly regard the novel as just this, we would still be wrong, wouldn't we? Because all it is, all it ever will be, all it ever can be, is an effort at saying how much you love your old man. And a day late at that.

Our visits are always so short.

30

It had drizzled that morning, but by lunch it was sunny and hot. We were all crouched on the brink of something, ostensibly the bank of the little pond on the grounds, but we knew it was much deeper than that. Mrs. Klink blushed painfully when she discovered that her skirt had been hiked very high up her wrinkled thigh and that Sheldon Cohen had been appreciating the view. Oh, don't cover it, he said in a sweet way that did little to make her feel better or less conspicuous, though it was clear to me that she was enjoying herself. Maria Cortez said, Take a pill. And then we were all quite quiet. I had just revealed to my friends that one of the keys in my possession was to the pharmaceutical locker. Emily Kuratowski was not with us that day. She had been taken to the hospital with pains in her side, this after having to wait hours before an orderly came to help her to the toilet. They're going to kill us all, Sheldon said, one by one. We're near dead anyway, Maria Cortez said. That's right, I said, that's right.

31

Teufelsdröckh was set on thirty well-watered acres adjacent to a suburban calamity called Calabasas, a roadside mishap that stank of fast food and automotive puke. It was a better buffer than the chilling water that surrounded Alcatraz, for at least the water promised certain death. We residents, as we were called, discarding the more unpleasant designation *patients,* as well as the more accurate term *inmates,* were not discouraged from venturing out to play in the traffic, as it were. We were free to walk or catch the bus that was twenty minutes late regardless of one's arrival at the stop. I walked three long, unshaded blocks to a mall the size of a small Iowa town. I had of course been in such places before, perhaps many times, though I had always tried to avoid them, so I should not have been surprised, stunned, by its massiveness or by the eerily familiar repetition of shops or by its complete uselessness in the face of its terrific promises. All I wanted was a locksmith, not even that, but a human with a key-making machine, my key on one side and a blank key on the other, a whirring, screeching noise, a spinning, buffing noise, and then two keys hopefully capable of opening the same lock. After exhausting myself with a walk the length of the place I learned by way of a directory map that Frenhofer's Key-Ask was located near the door through which I had entered. The Key-Ask was in fact a kiosk set in the flow of traffic and it was manned by a boy dressed in all black wearing black lipstick.

Are you Frenhofer? I asked.

Are you stupid?

Yes, but that is beside the point. Is this the Key-Ask?

That's Key-*Osk*.

Of course it is.

It's a pun.

If you say so. I'd like copies made of these keys.

His name tag read NICOLAS POUSSIN. He looked at the keys. A couple of these keys say *Do Not Duplicate.*

I realize that. That's why I want only copies of them. Do you always obey rules? You don't look like someone who follows all the rules.

Why do you say that?

Just something about you, a kind of death thing.

You're really giving it a tug, aren't you? Okay, I'll make them.

Just like that?

Just like that. To advance your story. Tell me, old man, what are these keys to, eh?

One fits a closet full of controlled substances.

Cool. He paused at the very old key. I can't do anything with this ancient thing. Is it real?

I don't know. Let me have that one. He took the old key off the ring and handed it to me. I put it in my pocket.

His tag now read JAN MABUSE.

Jan Mabuse paused at the last and smallest key. This key is beautiful, he said, and as he said it the traffic around the kiosk slowed or at least appeared to slow. This key is perfect. He hesitated, as if afraid to attempt duplication of the last key, which was in fact the key to the drug cabinet, but he could not have known that.

I spoke to him, told him that the perfect key, like anything perfect, was but mere shadow, apparition, wraith. I told him that Orpheus should never have looked back. I studied his paint-darkened lips and said, Make the key.

His tag now read: FERNAND LÉGER. He made the key, with the whirring, screeching, and buffing that I had wanted.

He did not charge me for my copies. He instead put down his protective goggles and prepared to leave. I asked him where he was going. He told me he was going home. No more keys for me, he said; his tag read CLAUDE LANTIER.

32

Sensuality, or more precisely lust, is the nonpareil Petri tureen for the breeding of ruinous and catastrophic miscalculation. I knew that, it having been a lesson I learned early in my so-called adult life, and so modeled my behavior, regarding all dealings with love and or lovers, actual and potential and imagined, on a robot I once saw in a movie when I was twenty-seven. I had smoked quite a bit of pot and the character might well have not been a robot, but I remember him as a robot nonetheless and his unfeeling and distant approach to matters of the heart seemed just about right. So, even though my short-afro-ed night nurse, her name will be now Clarabelle, made my heart flutter, or was it my medication, or worse? and even though she caused me to assemble a montage of some of my more fondly remembered erections, I did not and would not trust or confide in her completely. She had after all been intimate with Harley and loneliness and self-loathing can only explain so much. She had, on a purely animalistic plane, a plane worth noting and visiting, somehow bridged that experiential gap between the discrete and the continuous, between the distinct actuality of past conditions and the ephemeral, expanding, enduring, and untouchable attachment to those conditions, states of affairs, cases, hard-ons.

She was standing authoritatively behind her station desk, was Clarabelle. Her light-green smock covered with pastel smiley faces and the V-slit of her collar pointing seductively down to her, I assumed, nonexistent cleavage. I had already placed the original set of keys at the far edge of her desk and I believe she had pretended not to see me do it.

Finally, she looked at them. I wonder where those came from.

What?

Those keys.

Oh.

Are they yours?

Not mine.

Sarah, Sarah, are these your keys?

Not mine?

Anthony, are these yours? Clarabelle held them high and jingled them.

Nope.

I guess the owner will turn up, she said. She put them into her drawer.

Do you believe in time travel? I asked her.

I guess not.

It's just as well. Apparently, given that the occurrence of time dilation, whether based on velocity or gravity, doesn't allow backward travel, we could only hope to get you as old as me and that would sort of defeat the purpose, wouldn't it?

You're an interesting man.

I was once, I think. I'm pretty sure I thought so then. More fool me.

You know, I really don't like Harley, she said.

I nodded. I wondered if she thought that was supposed to make me like her more. I nodded some more.

What do you see when you look at me?

This was a great question and it took me completely off guard. I looked up at the fluorescent tubes on the ceiling of the hallway. I see a river in Iowa, I said. The first place I saw my wife naked. All we did was swim that day.

That's sweet.

I'm a sweet man.

33

I

My first self-conscious attention to a heading. I. A pronoun denot-
ing the self. Me. It is also the letter representing an imaginary
unit in math, the unit that lets the real number system extend
to complex numbers. Me. I'm sorry, my best and favorite lover
said to me, you are imaginary. I suggested that she multiply me
by i and give me another look and try. But all of this to prolong a
deferral, right?

I could see Billy fishing in some far-off stream or pond even
though I did not know if he liked fishing or had ever fished in his
what I imagine to be staid accountant's life with his daughter beside
him teasing him about something or another perhaps the way he
said the word *apricot* and there he was reeling in empty hook after
empty hook happy because his girl was there with him and maybe
his wife but wasn't it odd Billy thought there by that stream or pond
how when a child dies all other relationships seem so so so dismis-
sible forgettable shallow though he knew that she must have been
around perhaps in a backyard garden with an older or younger version of their daughter she teasing her mother about the fact that
she wore her rubber boots on the hottest and driest days but Billy
was with his daughter and then he was not but instead lying deader
than dead against that bank his arms and legs akimbo his eyes open
and lost-looking in the bright sun because there was no heaven no
stream no daughter to revisit though someplace along that stream
bank that riverbank she lay like him so so so still veins and arteries
and curious things-closed all kisses having been blown up a skirt
hiked up just over her knee her hands looking like they had wrung
the last water from a towel pots and pans piled up the bank waiting
for Billy to wash after the last dinner the last supper conjuring that
lie of a story where that Iscariot guy did the brave thing and pointed
out a toga-clad Jimmy Swaggart to the goose-stepping authorities

and some others who were tired of reading letters from living souls who had ceased or failed ever to recognize the difference between hopes and lies. So blow me a kiss sweet Jesus Billy said and I will let it light on my ass and my daughter will remain skirt-hiked-dead on a shore and friends will make tea make tea make tea and then visit in the cold dark of night Point Dume

And then there was you, me, us, red and black in the evening light lost to the wearing of hats and eager to return to stories that used to make some sense eager to recall easily demarcated boundaries of identity and designation and eager to resketch the likenesses of faces that were either familiar or desired wanting in the darkness of the wee hours which were no smaller than the rest to smell cooking that promised to free all of us from the chains of understanding yes ourselves and all those we loved or hated sought or dismissed the beautifulest of all visible things the lightning strikes of summer the stars the nebulae the nebulæ for only etymology's sake some sea tempest and thus awaiting in an alley then to that day with a vacant hugeness of loss looming we counted our weapons one of us anyway and aligned with our comrades and lined the halls with maps of our plans and stretched all things to their limits the budding disleafing and felling of trees notwithstanding my skull a great blue vault with eyebrows and anger in its large awkward gianthood rustling like some human noise in a forest a howling wind with no place to go a Brobdingnagian with a clumsy ham-fisted gait pretended to seek refuge while raising a hammer stood in a doorway prepared to fight in rude corridors and terrible closets and on beaches from which south extended until it stopped left unexplained left untouched left strange like a glance through a glass pane without a frame without an agent for beauty is a witch and did not we feel it so that the wretched made for lousy company not cheerful at all while hell and purgatory and paradise blended like clay on one spinning table upon which also rested my peaceable disposition until rough and then far rougher weather upset that temperament and forced me into that perplexing jungle that deep root-riddled tangle of wilderness that was myself

In similar fashion he came to some comprehension of the whole ballet, language being a small window through which very little passed and became helpful, the dance being nearly everything.

34

A pea can be chopped up and reassembled into the sun.

Emily Kuratowski had in life been married to a mathematician, she liked to tell people. She had been one as well but seldom mentioned that. She told me once that she had spent her life working on projective limit topology and canonical projections and she even tried to explain it a bit to me, but my glazed-over look made her smile politely and pat my twenty-year-younger head. That is why I don't think about these things anymore, she said. I would rather eat cherries and think about the wind. Emily was what kids in my day used to call walleyed, but was called later lazy eyed. In her case her left eye pointed slightly out and so she suffered exotropia. She and I talked about that and I told her that the condition sounded more like a nice place to visit. She told me that her husband had worked on ring theory. I didn't understand his problem and neither did he, she said. And none of it served him in life. He died bitter and, finally, unsolved. She picked up her yellow cup from the tray in front of her and drank through the bendable straw. I'm feeling a little better now. God, I hate this hospital.

Emily had money problems, stemming, she told me, from her inability to balance a checkbook. Oh, I can explain the Hausdorff maximal principle or Banach-Tarski paradox, but don't ask me to subtract seven from twelve. My husband was even worse, insofar as he had his head stuck so far up his ass he could smell his own breath.

You must have loved him, I said.

I suppose I did for a while. Then we just got wrapped up in life and work and love and the idea of it just fell away.

That's sad.

If it hadn't been for my constant affairs it would have been.

I laughed.

He never noticed. He never could have noticed. He never would have wanted to notice. If he had noticed, it wouldn't have mattered. He wouldn't have understood.

Too much in the clouds?

Too stupid. Thank god we never had any children.

I thought you had a daughter.

I do.

Oh. Just how old are you, Emily? My question came off as indelicate, I think, but she didn't mind.

I'm ninety-nine. Palindromic ninety-nine. At this age I look the same coming as I do going. And before you ask I have no sentimental or egotistical desire to reach one hundred for the mere sake of doing it. One hundred is not a terribly interesting number. In the Qur'an there are ninety-nine names for Allah. That's a funny thing for a Jew to know, isn't it?

We end up knowing all sorts of funny things. Imagine how many of them we forget in a lifetime.

Or two.

Or two.

35

The dining room was quiet and then quieter when Harley and his henchmen walked in. They made their noises and stood like weeds near the salad bar. Harley smiled. So, the keys have turned up, he said. I'd like to know who took them, but I guess that's not going to happen. Anyway, thank you. But know that I am still angry. This is my kingdom. He rocked there on those words for a prolonged moment, then repeated, This is my kingdom. He walked out, his workers on his pheromone trail.

I looked at the faces in the room. None was terrified, but none was happy. They had all come to terms with the idea and the reality of death, but a change in the suffering along the path to death was unsettling. At their ages, they had a right to expect routine, even in pain, even in torment.

The regional inspector is coming tomorrow, Sheldon whispered to me.

The feckless, perhaps shiftless, certainly slothful regional inspector made four visits a year to our facility. If he was not somehow profiting from whatever the Gang of Six was about, then he was at least so incompetent that a complaint to him would prove meaningless. Also, the residents were just too intimidated by Harley and his thugs to be seen speaking to him. Yet, for some reason, beyond me and probably any sane person, I was going to have a conversation with him. Just looking at him, in his plaid jacket and chinos and oversized metal-framed glasses, I imagined him with his father, a hidebound pedant without knowledge of man's nature or of a boy's, giving lesson after lesson to this dutiful dolt, in some dead language of morality. In other words, he was a Christian, and not the good kind. He was a spit-hurling, brow-raking participle grinder. How are we doing? What are we eating today? Speaking of sleeping, are we sleeping well and doing our exercises and going here, there, hither, and yond?

We've got a problem, I said to Finley Snerd. I kid you not.

We're having a problem?

Yes, some of the orderlies are abusive.

I'm seeing the problem. You're telling me that some of the order-lies are abusing the residents?

That's exactly what I just told you. I refused to be sucked into his participle gurgling vortex. We were sitting rather conspicuously at a picnic table on the lawn and I saw the brute Leon see us. He nod-ded his monster's head.

What sort of abuse are the residents experiencing?

Neglect. Mental and emotional ill treatment. I suspect there is some extortion.

I'm listening and telling you that these are serious allegations.

I am aware of this.

Are you willing to name names?

Harley, Leon, Ramona, Tommy, and Billy. And let me not forget Cletus. I'd like you to write this down, all of it. They killed William Marshall.

You're telling me they were responsible for him dying?

That's what *killed* means.

Keep going.

They attacked his room, his life. They damaged a photograph of his deceased daughter, it was very special to him, an extension of his being, and that upset him so much that he moved too quickly, fell and hit his head.

Snerd thumbed through a folder, pretending to look at notes. I'm understanding that the orderlies were searching for some miss-ing keys.

That's what they claimed. What would ninety-two-year-old, nearly blind William Marshall want with the orderlies' keys?

The regional inspector sighed. Well, I'm making note of all of this and we'll be getting back to you. I'm assuming you won't be mind-ing if I'm popping in sometime so that we can continue chatting.

They are going to kill all of us and I want you to write that down. Would you write that down, please?

Okay, I'm writing it.

And date it.

I'm dating it, as per your request. He closed up his folders and packed up his briefcase. He offered me his spongy hand to shake and I shook it. Well, I'll be going now.

36

Dear Son,

I received and read your letter of 30 May with great interest and I am sorry to be slow with my response. Thank you for it. Your letters are a staple of my continued soundness. I had hoped that my missive before yours might have allayed your concerns and fears, but I was evidently wrong. You appear to be as seized with panic as ever regarding my current state of affairs, but such obsessing serves neither of us. It hinders you from functioning properly, comme il faut, in the world and so undermines and negates my life's work as a father. So, cut it out. The orderlies are disorderly and let's leave it at that.

If there were others left in our family, I might write that they do not know me or that they have a wholly erroneous picture of me. This, whether they be brother, cousins, or grandchildren. Do not take the last in that list as a request or complaint. That ship has obviously sailed.

About my brother, your uncle. I envied him his life, simple and uncomplicated in its way. It perpetually seemed to me full of passion, if not love. Who knows which is better, or preferable. I would opt for the latter, but that is no doubt my artistic sensibility and penchant for the masochistic. But what does that leave one at the end? Some photographs? A few familiar tunes and scents? His death even seemed undemanding, easy, and uninvolved. All I have is involvement.

I do not expect another visit from you. I'm not crazy. That ship sailed with the other one. Not that I don't believe you would like to be here, but, you know, physics, geometry, and all that. Time simply is not with us. We are out of time. I realize that one can read that in a couple of ways. I choose it to connote out of sync, as if my choice matters, and in the end just what is the difference?

Throughout my life I have found myself several times in so-called dire straits and I did not despair. Not so much because I was or am an optimist, but because I am prone to asking myself the question, just how bad can things really be? So, I ask you to not despair either; it is a little late for that.

At my age, with so many measures having been taken and being taken, no measures really seem extreme. It's too bad, because sometimes extreme measures are called for. Extreme or not, measures have been chosen, if not yet employed. I remember hearing the cliché that one should not throw out the baby with the bathwater; that seems exactly the time to do it. But again, I am just Alice arguing with Humpty Dumpty.

The role of all this last act, as it were, is to provide a context for the impossible, a home for the contradictory, a bed for the irreconcilable. What I have planted, am planting, are like rhizomes, easy to put in, but you have to divide them before you know it. So much work. Come what may, we will do what we do and we will not stop or even pause for subversion or inversion.

All for now. I doubt we will see each when all is said and done, but who knows, really? Don't pick up any wooden nickels.

Love,
Dad

37

Still, it was not all clouds and gray skies—there was some sunshine. As with Maria Cortez, who looked as if she had been soundly fucked. She sat beside a smiling Sheldon Cohen and so I knew that all of it had been more than mere bragging. They appeared casual and quite comfortable in the, shall we call it, the slipstream of their activity, the two of them naively trusting that they shared a secret. Well, Maria naively thought so, as everything in Sheldon's posture and movement, he might as well have worn a display of bright feathers all around, was a betrayal of confidence.

Still, in spite of what I thought was rather barefaced and transparent, the fact of it was so incredible as to leave most, if not skeptical, then befuddled. I chose, quite reasonably, not to imagine the liaison and preferred to call it, in the privacy of my own head, though I did not consider it for any length of time, a bit of extracurricular activity. Of course, at their ages anything but using the toilet and going about the business of dying was extracurricular. If anyone had given Maria a cigarette, she would have smoked it happily. And I felt happy for her. And for him, however grudgingly. The two had just come wobbling and strutting, respectively, into my kitchen. Mrs. Klink was already seated with me, nursing her ubiquitous cup of green tea.

What's wrong with the two of you? Mrs. Klink asked.

Nothing, nothing at all, said Sheldon Cohen.

Maria Cortez giggled, maybe chortled; I have never known the difference. She sat next to Mrs. Klink and stared out into my living room.

Emily Kuratowski was still in the hospital but was scheduled to return to us the next day.

Emily does not look well, said Mrs. Klink.

She's ninety-nine, I said. She looks beautiful.

She's a hottie, said Sheldon Cohen.

To a considerable degree, by the time we have reached a certain age, it varies for each of us, we have said all we meant to say. Everything else is either a reissue or an elucidation, a gloss. Some utterances might be reconstructions of some erased pages, palimpsests of sorts, but it's mere repetition. There might even be supplement here or there, but our questions will have nothing more to seek but the texture of our texts, the colors of our recollections, but there will be no new colors and there will be no new tastes or sensations. The only new thing will be cessation, suspension, conclusion, and besides that we will have nothing to play with but the play within the shadows of whatever metaphors loom or we choose to have loom.

So there really was nothing for Sheldon and Maria to say and they said it. And so did Mrs. Klink in asking her question and so did I by sitting there and remembering the dream that I had, wondering if it was a memory.

In the dream I was back in the break room of the orderlies, the stolen keys already in my pocket, and I was hidden in the shadows of the lockers. I looked to the window that would be my escape and listened to the sickening huffing and panting of Harley and Caledonia or Clarabelle or Cissy or whatever I had decided to call her and on that same wall was a door, an old-fashioned wooden door that did not seem in keeping with the vintage or style of the building or any building on the campus. In my pocket was the old key. I had not placed it back on the ring with the others before leaving them to be recovered and it now occurred to me that this key might be important, that this key might be key. But the really strange thing about the door was that there was no corresponding door on the outside of that wall. I looked at the faces of my friends. They did not know that I was ever in the orderlies' break room. They knew only that Billy and I had somehow come to have possession of the keys that had caused us all so much trouble. I would tell them about the door. What would it mean to them? What did

it mean to me? I was not sure I had even seen the strange door I
thought I recalled.

Deep, long past halfway, into the journey of my so-called life, I
found myself in darkness, without you and you and you and you, a
whole list of you, and stuck on this crooked trail, the straight one
having been lost, and it is difficult to express how in this darkness,
rough and stern, as bitter as death, but what I saw, what I saw there,
out of slumber and wide-awake in that dark place, was the termination of some world and the beginning of another, a mountain
maybe, a wind pressing against me, issued from some sea I could
not see, and so I fled onward, thinking how lucky are the amnesiacs, when a panther addressed my presence and then a lion and
then a love long lost, all three heads uplifted, but the last of them,
she brought upon me much sadness, the kind that comes with fear,
and she wept with me despite her hunger and we were cast back
into some light, away from the cats, and I met a man whose silence
was well practiced and he recited to me his lineage and I did not
care and he told me he was a poet and about that I cared even less
and he told me he would travel with me and then I was impressed.
Who will be my Virgilius now?

   This was how I thought as I dragged my sorry ass across that
lawn, toward that wall, to that window and back to the orderlies'
smoke-sour break room.

38

Sometimes stories come and stop and go
Sometimes stories stop and go and go
Sometimes stories come and stop and come
Sometimes stories stop and stop and stop
Sometimes stories come and come and go
Sometimes Sometimes Sometimes come

Swing an ax at my head, brother Billy, brother Billy
Swing an ax at my head, brother Billy mine
Swing an ax at my head, brother Billy, brother kill me
Swing an ax at my head for I haven't got the time.

A pistol in the first act and all of that. I could hear the plaintive cries of juvenile crows most of the time in that late summer. I wondered when the cries would mature. Would they one morning be the sounds of adult crows or would the change come in the middle of the caw? Would that adult sound be approached? There it is, there it is, almost, almost there, ahhhh, there it is. However it is, so it is with age. And when do two things that are in fact the same thing converge and negate any notion of their ever having been anything but one thing? When does Cicero become Tully? When does the morning star become the evening star? When does nobody in particular become nobody at all?

If I am to create you, me, them, or you create me, you, them, then you or I have to do something to allow that making, so that there is making, making, almost there, made. As long as an individual is traced out only in repose, in some milieu, its, his, her critical qualities and essential attributes can only be stated but not created. A lesson I learned from god in that story about the first and loveliest, and no doubt overly tended, garden. It was one thing to have A and E (possibly universal and existential statements, respectively) lying about, but finally somebody's got to fuck up or fuck somebody or fuck the wrong somebody. Then you've got yourself a story. Then you've got yourself a world.

This whole business of making a story, a story at all, well, it's the edge of something, isn't it? Forth and back and back and forth, it's a constant shuttle movement, ostensibly looking to comply with some logic, someone's logic, my logic, law, but subverting it the entire time. Like a good little wog. But, eh, don't listen to an old man. I'm firing semantic blanks or, at least, filling them in. My son would laugh right about here. Or I would. Why do anything? That's what I keep asking and then I remember I said to my son, or he said to me, that it's not what you've made that will give you peace, that the only thing you get to take with you is having made it. Blah, blah, blah.

Sometimes I think about these things and I am taken back to my childhood. I perceived much of it as boring or painful, but that is growing up, isn't it? I spent most of my time attempting to pass beneath the worrying radar of my mother. True that one cannot complain about such worry in any concrete way, but it was annoying and, more often than not I feared, a function of her narcissism rather than any real selflessness. Photographs of me then show a youth with red, tired eyes, not quite sullen but numbed eyes, perhaps. Boredom was my worst enemy, but not the kind that sprang from idleness, as I read and wrote quite a bit, but from a nagging lack of engagement with the world outside my thoughts, stricken every day by a tenacious noonday devil who would whisper from my shoulder that I should return to the sad, torpid world, as if I was some hermit who had left it. I ignored the devil then because he seemed too poorly informed and dressed; I had never been allowed to actually join the world. But then I did, first by climbing into it, then by walking into it until it was over my head and lungs, and a world with the *world* turned out to be as boring as a world without, only with more embarrassing moments and better jokes. The world seemed to me suited to people who smoked cigarettes, for they appeared to create their own weather.

Still 38

Emily was in a wheelchair and that was where she should have
been. Still, without being bossy, as that was not her nature, she got
to wherever she wanted to go, and I was the one pushing her. She
was not faring well and it was clear that her being lost in her head
featured a return to her craft, namely, logic, and so she seemed to
speak in riddles. As when she said to me while I poured my cup of
tea, You would do well to remember Zermelo's theorem.

I'm certain that's true, I said to her. And what does that theorem
state?

That every set can be well ordered.

Well ordered?

A set is well ordered if every nonempty subset of that set has a
least element under the specified ordering.

A least element?

An element that is less than or equal to any other element in
a set.

And so it went. I hoped that when dementia settled in on me
that I would be as obscure and as interesting as Emily Kuratowski.
So it went, until one morning she asked, Are we going? I ask because I am not afraid.

You're not.

You should not be either. Make it what you want. Make it exactly
what you want.

I nodded. Then I will not be afraid either, my friend.

39

The exterior wall in the orderlies' break room. Turns out it was real after all and I held the ancient key that would open it. Emily Kuratowski sat in her wheelchair beside me, she having confessed to being sent by you to escort me through the door and, well, I might as well stop here. Emily is stopping me here, mainly because she refuses to be called a Virgil and because she, as I, we, simply cannot bring ourselves to play dumb enough to entertain any business about the circles of hell or about eternal torment, punishment, restraint, or whatever bugs and annoys the Christian souls that love to read Dante over and over. We will not pass through limbo or Limbo (is it a place with a proper name?), will not climb up and over any hairy-backed demons, wrestle with she-wolves, chat with Horace and Ovid, take joy in watching the anguish of our evil enemies. Nice poem, is all I'll say. But hell? Abandon hope, all who think there are gates. We will only acknowledge that there is a door and then realize, rather rightly, that it is not set into that exterior wall but leaned up against it, waiting to be taken home by some simpleminded employee, probably Harley, who no doubt needs a door to hell in his basement, or maybe by Leon, who needs really big doors.

So, why are we standing here? Emily Kuratowski asked. Rather, why are you standing? I'm sitting of course.

Because tomorrow is my birthday, I said.

How old will you be?

Seventy-nine.

A baby.

What will they do to us if they find us in here?

They'll ask us why we're here.

What will you tell them?

I'll tell them that we were wondering why they are such failures as human beings and that we were wondering also how such people live.

We're anthropologists.

Of a kind.

Why did you bring me here? she asked.

A moment of weakness, I said. Sometimes fear can make you creep into one camp or another, can make you almost believe what you want to think you're too strong to believe. I wanted to think there is a hell. I guess I wanted to think there is a heaven. I wanted to think that I would see my son again.

That's not a bad thing to think.

I shrugged. It's a stupid thing to think.

I cannot argue with that.

Do you think there is evil in the world?

I don't know what that means. I think there are people who are cruel. I know there are. What about you?

No evil.

Good?

Oh, there's good. No evil. No god or gods or devils? If there is a god, he's not very good at much.

What about meaning?

Meaning? You mean, like, purpose?

Okay.

She shook her head.

I nodded. Justice?

Maybe. Justice happens just often enough that the myth of it persists. Funny how injustice doesn't create its own mythology.

Hope springs eternal.

Hope.

Do you think we're in hell right now, this place?

No.

That was simple.

Hell would be if I'd never seen the Sieve of Eratosthenes as a child or if I had never been able to understand Gauss's *Disquisitiones Arithmeticae*. For you it would have been never reading *Huck Finn*. I'm guessing.

Close enough. So, we're not in hell now?

However much it feels like it.

But that doesn't mean we can't make it hell for someone else.

If I were twenty years younger, I'd kiss you.

If you were twenty years younger, I'd let you. Shall we get out of here?

Emily Kuratowski nodded. On our way out, she sneezed and then said, The axiom of choice does not apply if there is a finite number of bins.

Of course, I said.

40

It had been my experience that the one thing thieves hate more than anything else is theft. And so Mrs. Klink and Maria Cortez and Emily Kuratowski and Sheldon Cohen and I took all of our valuables, as they were called, and hid them away behind my azalea bush. And then we, in turn, went to the building administrator and told her that we had been robbed. The administrator, as she was called, had no face and so she could have no expression when one or all of us came to her with our reports. She made notes and said what she would whether she was being told a faucet was dripping or a chicken bone was caught in the throat of a wheelchair-bound, blind man, I'll see what I can do. This came as no surprise to us, but we made our reports nonetheless. We walked the hallways looking forlorn and lost, our lives' prizes had been stolen, our keepsakes, our memories. We stumbled into each other, we were so despondent. We cut sidelong and angry glances at the Gang of Six, whispered in the hallways that we knew who had done the pilfering—the bastards. It turned out that what upset a thief more than finding an empty mark was believing that he'd been beaten to the mark. My watch that you gave me, my watch that kept decent time if I checked on it now and again, a glance at the big clock on the street or called up that number that there used to be just to tell you the time, that watch with the sweep hand (does anyone still call it that?) that was stuck in a little circle, one of three circles, one of the other two was for the date and that I never used and the third I have no idea about, but perhaps it was the most important one, perhaps it not only kept track of time but kept time and if I had only looked at it, if I had only understood it and used it, I might have some years some days some hours left, but not for myself because I really don't need them, don't want them, and wouldn't know when to put them or keep them if I had them to keep or if I had a watch with a third circle that just happened to keep them for me. Rubato. My watch has been fake-stolen, I will call it, but interred under the dirt as it is, not rendering its readings to me, tick tick ticking through the anything-but-friable soil to the wormies and the buggies and the seedlings, it might as well be stolen, so is there any real difference, except for the time that is stored in those springs, caught in them, twisted in them, warped, buckled, contorted in the skinny housing that looked so elegant when you gave it to me, a watch like the one I had owned before and a watch very much like a new one that I might have bought for myself, but it was from you, wasn't it? And that made all the difference, all the difference when the leather wristband became stinky in the summer humidity, when sand would grind under it at the beach and I would wear it on and on because it was the time you have given me, time that just twiddled and peetled and staggered and tripped into the gloaming of everydayness, so that now my wrist feels so funny, outré, and not lighter, as one might expect, but denser, concentrated, like a head on Venus. My watch, your watch, sunk into the muck, laid to rest, inhumed with so much else, the wormies and the buggies and the seedlings and so much else, time, my time, because my time is all that's left, *my* nonspatial continuum, *my* measures of change in position and temperature and velocity, *my* sequences, *my* durations, *my* repetitions *my* repetitions, I agreeing with Leibniz (happily, because he had monads) and with Kant (sadly, because he was so damn predictable) that we cannot measure this *time* and therefore we cannot travel this *time* and therefore we're fucked and I'm an old man, so I can talk like this, say, say words like *fuck* if I want to, if I choose to, if the feeling moves me, if I have time for it, from time to time, but thank god and the devil for time, because if we didn't have it, well, things would just stack up, wouldn't they? Seconds piled on top of seconds on top of minutes on top of hours, with no place for them to go. What a mess. And this talk of eternity, it just won't last, and besides, what an awful place to meet. I would rather count the hairs on a cat, the grains of sand in a desert, the lies America has told the world, than admit that eternity makes any sense. So, we buried a few things.

41

To save power in those late-summer months Teufelsdröckh's turned off the air-conditioning an hour earlier and extinguished three of every four fluorescent panels in the corridors and so the evenings were warm and eerily lit, the flickering panels struggling to carve out small regions of shadowy light. By morning all the oldsters were shivering because to cope with the warmer early evening they had opened their windows and by daybreak the rooms were frigid. I never minded it so much, but it was no fun stumbling out in the mornings to be surrounded by bundled-up, yawning, and complaining residents of Limbo. Still, I was happier than I had been for my hours spent with my mathematician friend, her periods of hazy vacation and arithmetical flights of decampment notwithstanding.

You know what would be nice one of these evenings? I said.

A thunderstorm, Emily Kuratowski said immediately.

You've been reading my mind.

Or you mine.

Maria Cortez had told us at breakfast that she suspected someone had rummaged through her things again. But of course they found nothing, she snickered.

Emily and I were watching Harley and Tommy, involved in an animated discussion down the hall. I could not make out any of what was being said, but Tommy was scuttling left, the only way he scuttled, his head bent low, still high above Harley's, but his posture was of contrition, if not fear. I could imagine the dialogue.

You didn't find anything? You went through all of Kuratowski's drawers? What do you mean you didn't find anything? Harley glanced down at us and though I had a momentary fear that he was singling me out with his stare, he was not.

Nothing. And yes, I looked through every one of her drawers. It was like she'd been robbed blind.

Somebody around here is up to no good.

Us?

No, somebody else. Ramona, I'll bet it's Ramona. She's a sneaky one. Leon's hands are too big. And that troll Cletus never had an idea in his life.

What about Billy?

Who?

Just then one of the day nurses, the only one with any balls, her name was Gladys, made much noise walking toward Harley and Tommy. You! she shouted. Do you know how to use a key?

Harley watched her. He had no power over her and so fell into his short body and found his nest.

It seems you can unlock and open a cabinet well enough, but the real trick, the important part of using a key, is reinserting it and locking the cabinet. Do you understand me?

Gladys might have been an ally save for the fact that she hated any one of us as much as she hated Harley and the orderlies. She simply did not want waves. She stayed in her glass-walled office and sat behind her desk, completely visible during her few hours at work, and, ostensibly, worked. She was like a fish in a bowl, rather a reclusive crab in a cave in a bowl. This is the one responsibility you have, she said. To lock the cabinet once you've taken out the medication. Do you think you can do that?

Yes, ma'am.

She turned her attention to the residents and smiled. Good morning, ladies and gentlemen. It's a bit brisk, isn't it?

42

I noticed one other thing, moreover, which struck me rather mark-edly and with a smattering of nostalgia, and that was that Harley's voice reminded me of the voice of a man who had annoyed and harassed me when I was a youth in college, when I had fancied my-self a radical, when I got high a lot, but the voice from back then was considerably more educated, maybe even refined, but perhaps not as musical as Harley's, not to suggest a mellifluousness in Harley's voice, but it was certainly more so than that of the blazon of a federal agent who hounded me, and even then I didn't believe it because he seemed too young, but they had to start somewhere, didn't they, in the shacks of backwoods Kentucky or in the public school system of New York City, they had to come from someplace and they probably did begin early, were sought out in their forma-tive years because of some observed proclivity or other, a knack for languages or a way with people, but probably something far more base and useful in law dumbforcement, meanness, cruelness, the ability to easily turn their gaze away from mistreatment and pain, and a large, set jaw that was good at chewing gum for hours on end and it was his voice that I was reminded of, how he would fol-low me down Thayer Street during a rain and drink coffee at Spat's while I tried to ignore him and talk to the waitress on whom I had a crush and I remember her well too, an American studies major of ambiguous racial extraction or derivation and even she was struck by how struck I was by the presence of my shadowy friend and his suit that might as well have been a sandwich-board badge and there I would sit trying to talk to the waitress, and I hadn't yet even met your dear mother, trying to ignore the walking, skulking badge. I thought that maybe the waitress liked me, but it was all too much. And so I never even got a date or her phone number and suppose I had, suppose I had written her number down the back of my re-ceipt, why, I might not have been interested when I finally did meet your mother or I might have been in a different place, maybe in a

commune in cold-ass upstate New Hampshire with a coven of racially challenged American youths, and that is why you might well
owe your actual existence to the government of this nation, because had they made up their minds sooner that I was not a threat
to national security and the American way of life, had they not been
there to cock-block my efforts with the cute waitress, then I might
be in New Hampshire yet, making backpacks and fanny packs out
of hemp and natural dyes, and I was just mere seconds away perhaps from becoming the reluctant dance partner of a much larger
man in some federal penitentiary or maybe a milder correctional
facility where they serve cake, as one night I turned the tables on
the big badge, shadowy man, managed to lose him on campus,
doing so by entering a basement washroom of a classroom building
and exiting from a high window, and after that I waited for him
outside, his body language told of his exasperation and anger, but I
followed him then, became the hunter and tailed him, as they say,
back to his modest apartment on, of all places, Federal Hill, a silly
and sad-looking walk-up next to a popular Italian restaurant, what
else, and I wondered briefly if he was really a badge after all and
then I saw him visited by other badges, they were either cops or
unsuccessful bankers, the cut of their suits being rough and just fit-
ted, and I had a difficult time imagining why this badge or any
badge or anyone would have any interest in me except that I was a
black man in America who could read and because I had traveled to
Cuba on a sailboat when I was nineteen, on a sailboat with some
partying white boys who I was certain were not being followed,
wherever they were living, but maybe that was enough to label me
a commie for life, a red, a pinko, an enemy of the state, and how did
I get here except a noticed and remembered timbre of a voice, not a
deep voice, in fact a bit high for a man, even though I don't suppose
there is any range that a man's voice is supposed to fall into and I
wouldn't suggest such a thing, especially not to that boxer who
used to annihilate his opponents in the first rounds of all his fights
until the geniuses of the sport figured out that he couldn't render

them unconscious if he couldn'tn't hit them and the guy got so frus-
trated that finally he bit off a piece of another fellow's ear, off, I
don't care how hungry I might have felt, I would never have done
that, but he was not an enemy of the state, had never read Marx,
though he was running around in short trunks trying to eat the
citizenry, no, but I was such an enemy and it was because I had read
Mao and Marx (Karl and Groucho) and Malcolm and I had been to
Cuba. But back to voices and back to Harley, who reminded me of
the big badge in no other way except that they were both white, but
that was hardly a shared attribute that was in any way defining, unless of course either one of them had been a heavyweight boxer
back then, now they're all large Russian fellows that eat rivets and
make tools from their fingernail clippings, and, like I said, you
weren't even, you know the expression, a twinkle in your father's
eye, in my pinko eye. The badge, his name was Wesley, I saw it on
his mailbox, I saw it and then I did a terribly foolish thing, I sneaked
into his apartment because I was certain he had been in my home
and I wanted to know a little something about the fucker, pardon
my Danish, and when I did sneak in, it was easier than it sounds, old
doors and all that and a key under the mat, I found him in mid-butt-
fucking session with another man, perhaps another badge, but it
was difficult to discern, what without his clothes and with him
frantically ducking for nonexistent cover, and because I stayed perhaps less than a second, well, at any rate, I personally didn't have a
problem with his sexual preference, but I'm certain that his agency
would have a problem with it, their using the don't-let-us-find-out-
we-won't-burn-you-at-the-stake policy, and so I never saw him
again and it was too bad because he was not an unattractive man,
unlike Harley, and after that I felt sad for him, hiding in that way,
worried all the damn time that someone might find out he was fond
of men's bottoms, and I imagined him later, having left the force,
living in Michigan maybe or Indiana and trying to carve out a life
in the home-security business and hiding from his clients the fact
that he lived with a man who was perhaps a designer of public foun-

tains, while Harley, ugly, grotesque Harley, invaded the open legs of that sweet little nurse and arched his appliance-shaped hairy back over her small frame like a camel-man and thumped away until he came and she finally collected her tiny white clogs and scampered down the dim hallway to later chat with me at the desk, without a stain on her smock, on her face, or even the slightest inclination to apologize to me for having sullied my image of her, but I could not have cared less, who was she to me after all, a pretty face. I was too old to be impressed or taken in by a pretty face or twenty pretty faces or two hundred but she had left that Harley back there in the break room, on that pathetic cot, that I had regrettably seen and so could picture, with circles of Pall Mall smoke coiled around his head like serpents, smiling and enjoying the coolness of the wet spot, and he glanced down at his glistening balls and beyond to his yellowed toenails and observed that they needed trimming, but waved off the major project, too much trouble, grooming, too much trouble, scratched his furry ass and gobbled up a few more villagers, gnawed on the heads of those below him and his enemies, wondered who was stealing his spoils before he could and I am sitting with Emily Kuratowski, my friend, and she is slipping ever further away, her eyes looking alternately cloudy and glassy more of the time, her voice, which is truly melodious, trailing off so much more often, Tychonoff's theorem states the Cartesian product of any arbitrary set of compact topological spaces is itself compact and many people say that this is an equivalent of the axiom of choice, but I just don't buy it, Zermelo's well-ordering theorem, yes, Zorn's lemma, yes, but not Tychonoff's, even when considering the proof of the existence of non-Lebesgue measurable sets, she says this and then comments on the zinnias, they seem a little droopy, and then drifts off toward a syrupy sleep, only to awaken and look me in the eye and say, We cannot let them live in peace, and I nod and lament that my poor friend's last lucid moments must be consumed with the cancerous worry over retribution and requital, but I can say that these goals are not attractive and not as strongly longed for by me, though I would claim that we are not vindictive or spiteful, we, I think, seek more to discharge equity, not so much to exact revenge as to satisfy justice, and I feel it is my responsibility, mission, to see her and my other friends satisfied in their final days and it comes as a two-pronged campaign, at once putting an end to the reign of the Gang and our taking control of what we have left, our exercising our power to act, the way I acted when first I met your mother, I've always loved that construction, *when first I met,* well, when first I met your mother I was in my late twenties, seems like just a thousand years ago, she was ostensibly white and I, as the badges pointed out earlier, was and remain ostensibly black and though it hardly seems to matter now, it did then, and the excitement of our difference and the electricity of our head-turning presence in certain venues, sometimes unexpected, the venues, not us, like in a little church in a podunk village in central Connecticut. We had wandered in to beat it out of a torrential rain, the hardest in fifty years we were told by the old custodian who couldn't stop staring at us, then again by the little nasty pastor who found us equally odd, hardest rain in a half century, I thinking that it could have simply been that they didn't understand what a beautiful woman like your mother was doing with a homely oaf like myself, but of course that wasn't it. I was born at night but not last night, as I heard a UPS man once say, and boy was that a relief, wherever you be let your wind go free who knows if that pork chop I took with my cup of tea after was quite good with the heat I couldn't smell anything off it I'm sure that queerlooking man in the porkbutchers is a great rogue I hope that lamp is not smoking fill my nose up with smuts better than having him leaving the gas on all night I couldn't rest easy in my bed in Gibraltar even getting up to see why I am so damned nervous about that though I like it in winter it's more company O Lord it was rotten cold too that winter when I was only about ten was I yes I had the big doll with all the funny clothes dressing her up and undressing that icy wind skeeting across from those mountains the something Nevada sierra nevada standing at

the fire with the little bit of a short shift I had up to heat myself I
loved dancing about in it then make a race back into the church
because the storm had started up again as suddenly as it had ended
and so we were caught there once more in the house of Jesus with
the pastor and the custodian and the holy spirit, until the pastor
asked your mother if her parents knew where she was, she did look
young, and I appreciated the pastor asking questions first and plan-
ning on shooting later, but still I didn't appreciate it one bit, and
neither did your mother, but maybe she did, maybe we did and it
gave our being together, our approaching union, a bit of that out-
law appeal. We left there, heavy rain and all, hail by now, I had
never been so wet, so thoroughly soaked, but we felt none of it, but
wandered as deep into the middle of that little depressed town as
we could go and we kissed there in the dead, and I mean dead, center of Podunk, Connecticut, the name of the town I can't recall,
maybe it's age, maybe it's something worse, maybe it's because I'm
making up my past just the way every one of us makes up our past
anew each time we visit it, what actually happens is always just a
dress rehearsal for what you will report later, but it was undressed
that your mother and I made you, if I can be so vain as to use that
term, *made*, but god didn't make you, nature didn't make you, if
we're going by cause and effect, then the big gay badge from Federal
Hill made you because I wasn't off living in a commune fucking an
art-school dropout instead of your sweet, blessed saint of a mother,
me, son, aye, yer mother was a saint, a fucking saint who had an
affair with that flyboy and even if she didn't, she still considered it,
lusted after him, but I loved her then and I loved her then and then
and then and even now though she left me before even you did before even you did before even you did before even you

43

But on the way back home tonight, you wish you'd picked him up, held him a bit. Just held him, very close to your heart, his cheek by the hollow of your shoulder, full of sleep. As if it were you who could, somehow, save him.

There was a rainbow over the hills to the north of campus. Maria Cortez stared at them. Gravity hates me, she said.

Gravity hates all of us, I told her.

I remember when gravity didn't give me a second thought.

It was just biding time.

I heard that Ramona was fired.

I looked around for Ramona and didn't see her. I saw Leon standing at the central building. He was wiping down a wheelchair, perhaps of someone who had died. He'd been wiping it for a good thirty minutes, nervously glancing about all the while.

I can't say I'm sorry to see her go.

The last I'd see of Ramona was when she and Harley were having an argument that tumbled with them into the dining room.

I know it was you, Harley said.

I have to clean Chen's toilet.

Leon and Cletus don't have the initiative and I know it's not Tommy.

I punched in at six just like every other day.

Just admit you've been doing stuff on your own.

What do you want to talk about?

I'm done with you.

Me? Me? You think I did it?

You might as well pack up. With that Harley stormed away.

Ramona followed. Billy, it must be Billy.

Who?

44

$$\sum_{i=0}^{\infty} f(i) = a$$

The question was whether there was some real value to which all of this, all our naming, thinking, speaking, breathing, wanting, loving, lusting, fearing, worrying, laughing, obsessing, liking, hating, changing, hindering, bringing, facilitating, curbing, retarding, tilting, running, sitting, looking, gazing, staring, listening, learning, ignoring, forgetting, misplacing, framing, distrusting, calling, naming, relinquishing, passing, entrusting, remembering, eating, drinking, sleeping, beating, hurting, contributing, basking, consigning, waking, stirring, losing, winning, drawing, informing, rigging, equipping, falling, disclosing, naming, administering, requiring, mustering, bathing, setting, washing, stalling, disguising, causing, ridding, masking, detailing, indicating, disposing, designating, clumping, breaking, counting, limiting, naming, eclipsing, assuming, flowing, tattling, tempering, flowering, veiling, dispensing, donating, teaching, helping, falsifying, disseminating, hurrying, dodging, naming, working, sullying, providing, succeeding, stonewalling, throwing, kicking, believing, uttering, serving, renouncing, attaining, venting, punching, treading, expanding, diminishing, devoting, hustling, stopping, dealing, allowing, qualifying, vacationing, showing, desiring, yearning, exploring, swearing, hedging, mining, raising, delivering, reneging, modulating, agreeing, betraying, naming, making, singing, whispering, exuding, burying, covering, occasioning, keeping, leaving, impeding, rising, clearing, deferring, sabotaging, executing, racing, balking, naming, stockpiling, sacrificing, distressing, coming, suppressing, slipping, inculpating, jacketing, shouting, lunging, frustrating, circulating, expressing, equivocating, flourishing, rotting, recoiling, repressing, emitting, impressing, collapsing, trusting, naming, thriving, trapping, pitying, depressing, convalescing, proffering, surrendering, renewing, hosting, slanting, stringing, ducking, knowing, deciding, lying, pussyfooting, challenging, doting, adhering, granting, hesitating, bequeathing, questioning, triumphing, obstructing, affecting, blocking, regarding, choking, grasping, delaying, inhibiting, shaping, milling, interfering, negating, reversing, revering, feeling, imploring, dipping, concocting, tergiversating, convincing, cherishing, naming, noticing, impugning, perceiving, camouflaging, arranging, tensing, evoking, sequestering, destroying, filling, sharing, healing, entwining, listing, steaming, petitioning, primping, separating, tainting, decentering, ambushing, refilling, becoming, sidestepping, sensing, emptying, steeling, calculating, identifying, smiting, converting, frolicking, achieving, adoring, refusing, dogging, constructing, clutching, stealing, extolling, quivering, faltering, menacing, imperiling, frothing, testing, abdicating, narrowing, opening, prospecting, directing, misunderstanding, judging, dividing, taking, producing, vacillating, hoping, indulging, tailoring, airing, atoning, sweeping, browbeating, repelling, surfacing, studying, reproducing, visiting, delighting, electing, copying, paralleling, creating, bracing, rattling, biting, reaching, taunting, functioning, obviating, gravitating, naming, turning, wavering, gambling, lapping, nailing, risking, discouraging, placating, divining, discerning, pushing, pulling, timing, preaching, spinning, yanking, processing, deducing, tracking, relying, lighting, preparing, referencing, stroking, understanding, substituting, facing, existing, portraying, moping, idling, furthering, sublimating, warning, hewing, darkening, petting, misdirecting, presiding, forcing, distancing, patting, rationalizing, alienating, elevating, putting, quibbling, caring, repairing, projecting, worshipping, apologizing, sizing, brownnosing, riddling, chancing, deploring, descending, prodding, skirting, orienting, asserting, gesturing, inserting, reducing, deserting, overtaking, righting, grating, echoing, fuming, torturing, insinuating, channeling, discounting, leaking, naming, diving, naming, practicing, deriding, continuing, sorting, laboring, interspersing, nodding, restoring, routing, situating, accounting, tightening, relaxing, doing, telling, occupying, uniting, ribbing, centering, releasing, revisiting, holing, pampering, losing, objecting, starring, appealing, doubling, positing, reviewing, giving, wobbling, referring, viewing, regulating, hooking, extinguishing, burnishing, encouraging, waffling, igniting, iterating, answering, reeling, naming, popping, recapitulating, shilly-shallying, dillydallying, refuting, disputing, blowing, tintinnabulating, conjuring, having, hunkering, rejecting, dithering, extending, undertaking, inhaling, exhaling, teasing, beating, scratching, defining, defaming, fooling, trimming, containing, cutting, nibbling, naming, attending, conforming, abiding, rerouting, lasting, taming, claiming, blaming, shaming, portaging, naming, ticking, kissing, tonguing, presuming, imagining, dreaming, graying, sectioning, lashing, jeopardizing, resting, meaning, testing, concluding, cresting, modeling, dragging, lifting, pickling, naming, inducing, tickling, slashing, licking, sticking, bounding, doubting, leaping, jumping, deeming, punctuating, naming, standing, tasting, spitting, swallowing, thumbing, fingering, naming, lounging, scrounging, hounding, resisting, clapping, waving, besieging, retreating, attacking, relenting, sucking, screwing, fucking, and naming, would lead to.

$$\sum_{i=0}^{\infty} f(i) = a$$

45

It was a small stage, but it was our stage, a kind of theater-in-the-round, we endlessly confusing each other with directions left and right and up and down, our backs always to our audience, our terrorists. Our terrorists had no names, no affiliations, would show up on no arrays of radar, and their insignificance in the world spoke grimly to our place in the world, even though the stakes of our performance were high, could not have been higher, and they, the stakes, were certainly not diminished by our temporal and physical proximity to that most supreme of all stakes. The fact that Billy was so old did not, would not, cause us to mourn his death any less, but no one heard us. The same with Dorothea Greene, Clarissa Madden, and Diego Jones. Considering the lost ones, the murdered ones, and the nature of administrative and familial reactions and response, the criteria for our selection became painfully obvious and glaring. We, each of us, subjected to the torment of the Gang of Six, had no one, no children, no friends, no spouses. We had outlived everyone and this was our reward, this was what we had found or what had found us.

Maria Cortez might have been smarter than all of us. Even after her interlude with Sheldon Cohen. She not only reported that her pearl earrings had disappeared one at a time and also her late husband's pocket watch with the relief image of a horse's head on the cover, but she told the floor administrator that whoever had done it left, on her dresser surface, three threaded needles.

Harley was hunched down on a pale-blue knee not too far away at the time of Maria's well-rehearsed and brilliant performance, complete with plenty of hand waving and stammering, ending with the true bit of genius, And the thread didn't even match any of my clothes. He was attempting or pretending to adjust the lower straps on a patient lift and his lack of reaction betrayed his seething anger. I could read his lips through the back of his square head, Leon, he said, Leon.

I followed as closely as I could or I should I did my best to keep up as Harley took his deliberate, appliance strides across the lawn, toward the central building. I went to the window of the break-room window and caught the ruler in mid-rail.

Don't lie to me, you overgrown, misshapen creature, you enormous hog with lips, you gorilla-mitted moron! Don't you lie to me!

But, boss, I . . . I . . . I ain't stole nothing without talkin' it over with you.

Then who's threading the damn needles!

Not me.

Do I look stupid to you, you hulking heap of hyperthyroidic heft, you bumbling bearish behemoth bedbug!

Hey!

Shut up!

Boss.

Shut up!

You don't have a brain in your head. It just can't be you. Somebody's up to no good around here.

Harley came to the window and peered out. I was plastered back-flat against the wall. It was broad daylight. I was just hoping no one would see me when someone saw me. It was Coco or Cecily or whatever her name was, the lovely night nurse on her way to her shift, and she was strolling across the green in her white clogs, shaking her tiny bottom, the late afternoon sun making her appear alluring, ghostlike. She saw me and she waved, not to or at me, but to Harley, who was calling out and making what he took to be alluring animal sounds and perhaps were. She observed me as clear as the ass on Harley's face but did not give me up or away or however that goes. Soon she was gone and I slunk off back to my rooms.

There I sat alone and fretted about what retaliatory measures Harley might take. It seemed clear to me that he suspected me and my comrades, but I was not certain of this and decided to not give myself or us away by either acting rashly or seeming nervous or wary. I read. I read Schopenhauer, perhaps as a kind of perverse self-punishment for something, I did not know what, but more for his sheer analysis of will and motivation. My friends and I had not articulated our final move, our finale, so to speak, but it was all too clear to us how everything must go. I turned a page and heard an administrator, oh those administrators, shouting at Harley for leaving open the pharmaceutical cabinet, Yet again! I heard this and smiled to myself and then bored myself into a deep and beautiful sleep by reading Zola's *Thérèse Raquin.* I dreamed troubled and dysfunctional French dreams about first cousins marrying and about controlling and narcissistic aunt, uncle, father, and mothers and about artists who cannot find their own pathetic and pitiful voices amid the noise of family struggle. I dreamed like that and was glad for it as I was bored into deeper and deeper sleep, lower and lower into the abyss of myself, down into the rooted, fathomless, subaqueous heart of my psychosis, my abstruse, mantic core, where I knew there was something to find, but knew I would never find it.

46

The moon was in full gloom outside my window while I watched Harley, Leon, and Tommy tear up my rooms. I remained calm, peaceful even, somewhat impressed by my own steadiness. Perhaps if you tell me what you're looking for.

Shut up, old man, this from Leon, who was markedly annoyed and choleric, he having been reamed and upbraided by his master. Funny how a good upbraiding can bring you down.

But I just sat there, my book in my lap, enjoying the clumsy display of their bodies. They really were stooges. As I watched them, as my fear of them was absorbed and shrunk by my newly realistic perception not so much of them but of myself. I was coming to understand that none of this was about them, none of our plans was meant to address their menace in our world. Our high and counterfeit hopes that we might save others from their evil drifted out my window into the gathering twilight. Our silly games with them had been fun, but just as the world discounted these ruffians, so would we, so did we, as, to a person, we all realized what precisely was at stake. By ridding ourselves of our keepsakes and so-called valuables before the approaching larceny, we had in fact shown ourselves how little anything material, regardless of sentimental and symbolic import, really meant. I was perhaps the last to know it, I being, if not the least bright, the least wise. I believed at that moment that, whether they could articulate it or not, my nonagenarian comrades had known all along just what it was we were doing, saying. Because finally every action is a statement, just as every utterance is an action.

Any of these books worth anything?

Yes, but in a currency you can't spend.

Here's a camera, boss. It's old.

It's a piece of shit.

Tommy threw the Leica across the room. It hit the wall.

47

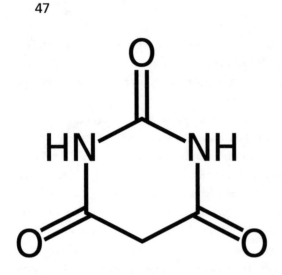

Sheldon Cohen was nonchalant as he browsed through the drugs closet. Usually he was ever so slightly fussy, if not on edge, but now, with me serving as sentry, in this space of vials, phials, ampoules, and bottles, he was completely at ease and in charge. He set the containers onto the counter and I stuffed them into my jacket pockets. Amytal, Seconal, Tuinal. He held a bottle close to his face. Ah, here we have it, Nembutal. And finally, Noveril and temazepam, that's a nice cocktail for any occasion.

48

The moon was bright. Stealing the van was not difficult. Half the time they were left running in a parking lot down the hill from the central building, perhaps to keep them cool. I never knew. Regardless, the keys were nearly always either in the ignitions or stashed under the mats. Who would steal one of those beasts with a chairlift? Certainly not a joyriding teenager, unless he was highly imaginative. I started the vehicle and moved up the circular drive toward the front of our residence hall. It was more like steering a boat than driving a car, the back end caught in crosscurrents and eddies. I felt as if I were shouting the command to stop to my first officer and he to the helmsman when I stepped on the brake; however, I did manage to come to a halt near enough to the entrance. Mrs. Klink, Maria Cortez, and Sheldon Cohen came slowly out and filed into the van. I got out and went to Emily Kuratowski's aid. She pushed herself out of her wheelchair and told me she would walk. Well, she couldn't, but she was so tiny by this time that even at my age I was able to carry her. All seated, we drove off campus and west. And this is where, this is where, this is where, normally, you would get a detailed description of our journey and it might go something like this:

I had never seen the moon so huge. I drove toward it and it grew, as if we were drawing nearer. We sang songs, songs we knew, songs we didn't. We sang:

My eyes are covered with sleep
I've walked through the years just fine.
Oh, I failed once or twice along the way,
But I got up every time.

The lights on the porches are dark
And no smoke from the chimneys rise.
Oh, the last time I checked my aching heart,
It was beating, to my surprise.

They let the dead bury the dead,
But they can't because they're decayed and blue.
Oh, the dead they are a lazy lot,
A hopeless, helpless crew.

We will live until we die,
Until then we'll scribble some lines
About how the dead greet us every day
And remind us of our crimes.

We'll listen with both ears.
We will watch them with both eyes.
Oh, the day their voices leave us alone
We'll begin to realize

That puzzles come and go,
That children laugh and cry,
That nature abhors a vacuum
And every truth will spawn a lie.

And then maybe we would have a bus crash and it might sound like this:

Shibocraishcruncruncsqirpopchiksanpcunkicripfissssclnterterchi chinkripdanfripbingchinriplashicrackripchikpoptapknicknocslith ingkascrippopsicbangabingafrangakripknitficrashshebinbangboo mbinggingfeshcaripcrazingfacrinkacrashcringsnapsnasnasnasna ppingcrumkarumvfuvfuvfuvfuvfuchinkfuck

But none of that here. We made it to Malibu and Point Dume. We even made it to the beach at the base of the promontory. I carried Emily Kuratowski. She seemed even lighter that time. We looked out over Santa Monica Bay, at the lights, at the water, at the moon, but mostly at each other. I might have been the only one who experienced an inkling of reluctance or irresolution, but it was only an inkling and I soon learned how small that unit is as it disappeared with one line from Emily.

I don't have to take the potion, I'm sitting on the sand at the beach.

I took the urn of Billy's ashes from the sack that Sheldon had carried for me and sat it with us.

This where normally you might get a lot of touching and sentimental language and portentous dialogue, but I don't think so. We took our medicine and then we sat with ashes.

VENUS

Speaking of *N*othing

A

> Coma, coma, coma,
> That's what I'm in, that's what I'm in.
> Coma, coma, coma,
> That's what I'm in today!
>
> Torpor, torpor, torpor,
> That's what I feel, that's what I feel.
> Torpor, torpor, torpor,
> That's what I feel today!

The great, splendid, useful thing about a character in a coma is that he can say just about anything. But why would he want to?

You're not in a coma.

Says you.

Here's what it looks like where I am right now:

I've always wanted to see this place. I can see there's a river
down there. I wonder if it's deep. Probably fast in places. I'm angry
with my education. I wish I could have come upon this landscape
with no knowledge. I wish I could have been simply hiking along

until I paused and shook my head and wondered, what is that ahead of me? Imagine the marvel of it.

It's beautiful wherever I look. I suppose that's to be expected. Or maybe not. What does it mean, this being beautiful? Is it really in the eye of the so-called beholder? Is it beautiful because of what it is or because of what it was? Is it beautiful to me because it speaks to age, to the passage of rivers and time and the erosion of so much? I could argue all day with an idiot who does not find this landscape beautiful, but even he can point to no place in it that is ugly, where I find it unpleasant to fix his gaze. Except perhaps for that one cloud, you see the one I mean. That one there. Yes. It might be a cirrus. What do I know from clouds? It might be a forming thunderhead. It might be the beard of god or one of the gods, the genital hair of the devil. What I love is that the distance is so distant. One can see all the way till one stops seeing, till it's dark, till the matter falls into other hands. There are more shadows than you can count, should one be a shadow counter, reckoning ghosts and totting up silhouettes, making a mark for each one in a little book attached to your belt by a string. Is it early or late? How sad to be late. Sadder to be late early. How wonderful to be late late. There is no vagueness, though nothing is distinct, a well-defined place with no definition. Pass the bottle. A bottle for me. A bottle for you. I'm taking a nap. I am just now letting myself go, with the lassitude produced by one disheartening, dispiriting evening of bad weather after another. Again, I would close my eyes if they weren't already shut. From this moment on I cannot open or shut my eyes. Hang me in a museum and I will be happy. Hang me in a mausoleum and I won't know the difference. Help me paint the charnel house, the charnel house, the charnel house. Help me paint the charnel house that's out on Drury Lane. Call this a profound state of unconsciousness. I cannot (or will not) be awakened, I do not respond to light (seems I never did), I do not have sleep-wake cycles (no such thing), and I do not produce voluntary actions (a matter open to debate). How romantic, this language about the depth of my depth, somewhere between here and Glasgow. They say I'm a ten. I don't know whether that is good or bad, but I know that it is irrelevant. I think I'll move a finger just to fuck with them. If I could get up and walk to the window, I would. If I could be fidgety and not remain fixed, I would. If I could stand over there and observe the fine rain that I heard someone mention, I would. The rain will stop soon. Then there will be a sweet sunset to which I will not bear witness, a sweet sunset, twilight, evening. A waning moon and it will rise toward midnight. And some words are so familiar. Here, at this juncture, I might recall the gaps in my stories or the gaps in your stories or I might realize, as I do, that the gaps are the stories and that I should stop trying to leap over them and instead into them, the gaps. By the way, burn me up when the time comes. That patch of ground is no patch at all; it covers nothing. That plot is nothing but another gap that gets filled in by itself. I'll be dead and so it will never be my plot, in part or whole. My brother was buried in one and it did him no good, did his children no good. They still pay him visits, like morons. Even his pretty wife continued to stop by his plot and retell his story, the parts she knew, the parts she remembered, until she too moved in beside him. He was only a moderately good man or so I understood from all reports. I did not know him well; that made him a decent brother. Still, he never stole anything from me, never betrayed me, never even hurt my fragile feelings. He never invited me to his grave, his plot. He never had the language he needed. I always had too much, maybe. Perhaps I only talked too much. Wending my way through words to find a plot worthy of either digging up or filling in, isn't that what it was all about? I probably would have nothing but truly fond feelings for my brother had he not had such success with his one book. He was a bibliographer. Someone has to do it, he would always say of his work, and he wrote a book that remains in print, *Famous Lines from Obscure Books*. I hated that book and I hated that he put a line from me in it. That I no doubt belonged in it was beside the point and it didn't sweeten the pot that he had acted in sober and diligent sincerity. The line occurs near the end of my *Pass the Joint, Motherfucker;* an extremely high character slaps his forehead and says, *Oh, that's what* epiphany *means.* Had he included me to poke me a little, to needle me, to annoy me, I could have easily forgiven him, and what's more I would have found him a more interesting person. He was what he was, uncomplicated, undemanding, somewhat unassuming though he was a bit pretentious, guileless (not at all a bad thing), and decent. He was completely unlike his brother, who would probably have fucked his French wife if given half a chance. One Thanksgiving in Iowa City, I did have half a chance. My wife had just come back from Canada and her fling with the flying boy, though she didn't know I knew, but I knew I knew and that was bad enough, and so our house was filled with tension and Irish whisky. It was typically and brutally cold that Thanksgiving. Anne-Charlotte being from Nice did not like the weather and pretty much refused to leave the house. I walked into the bathroom while she was just stepping out of the shower. I froze, staring at her. She was beautiful and, in her French way, knew it. Excusez-moi pendant que je me sécher, she said, but really wasn't asking me to leave. I felt like a hippopotamus in a canoe. I flatter myself thinking that she might have been willing to kiss me, but, regardless, I never found out. I backed out of the room like a coward, felt guilty for a few seconds, then thought to myself that she was worth seeing. My impure thoughts, if I actually had them, were apparently enough to let me feel even with my decent, bibliographical brother and nearly square with my indecent, flyboy-loving wife. It had been nice of my brother to come visit, though a surprise, as I was not the most pleasant person and certainly not a pleasant brother. When he arrived, I asked, Why did you come to Iowa City? He replied, Because this is where you live. Again, without a hint of irony or even an appreciation of his question begging. One night, after dinner, while we sat alone at the kitchen table drinking tea and Irish whisky, he asked me if writers were like composers. I, for one of the few times in my life, did not answer immediately but stared at my tea, in particular at a bit of leaf floating near the far rim. Finally, I said, No, we have no math. We cannot divide our words in half and achieve predictable tones. We have no relative minors. We have no circle of fifths, except for the ones we drink. As much as there is magic in music, what we make comes only out of magic. I was a little drunk, I realized. The tones of music are the tones, an A is an A, a B-flat a B-flat. But what is a ball? What is a game? What is a hell? This is kind of a hell, isn't it? Having to sit here and listen to me. He sipped his whisky. Why do you ask? I wanted to know. He said it was because he had just remembered how our notebooks were called composition books when we were kids. I drank all of my whisky and stared into his face. He could have offered no answer that was as beautiful or as sublimely disappointing. And as earnest as a whale's song or baby's cry. My brother was not without real faults to accompany the petty ones I chose to attribute to him. He was an alcoholic for much of his life and he claimed for a while that it was a disease and asked if I could be a little more compassionate and then he told me one extremely hot July night at his place in DC that he wasn't suffering from a disease at all, but that he really liked to drink and that was apparently not good for his relationships. Or your liver, I added. This from the man who wrote *Pass the Joint, Motherfucker,* he said. It wasn't about drugs, I said, somewhat stupidly. He laughed. Then he stopped drinking, whether it was cold turkey (his stopping) I don't know, but of a sudden he no longer had that sour smell, that idiotic glaze on his eyes. He was sober and to his credit he was sober without a god. He was more like he was before drink and this was good and bad. To say that I did not love my brother would have been not altogether true. In fact, I envied him. He saw a beautiful world. It was a fault, but an honest one. It was this childish disposition and my disdain for the optimism and hopefulness that provided me with the conceit that art must arise through suffering. Perhaps because of my own shortcomings, this manifested in my seeking to create that suffering in those in my circuit of life. My sin as a cynic was to take myself seriously. And so I pray you, by that virtue that leads you to the topmost of the stairs, be mindful in due time of my pain. Poi s'ascose nel foco che gli affina. Into the fire that refines. But do not take me too seriously, for I could not take that. Thank god there is no religion in my life, the fire notwithstanding. I noticed some time ago the disappearance of the sin of simony. So many Simon Magi about, I suppose. One could come in here now and lay hands on me and I'd twitch a toe or get an erection and make his career. But there will no wood showing in these parts. That's okay. I remember sex and I remember it fondly, but I cannot recall any singular sensation of any distinct and particular, discrete even, moment of the sex itself. I recall only the air around it, whether I was happy or sad, peaceful or distracted, falling into or out of love, the excitement of anticipation, disappointment. I can talk myself into imagining that I remember especially fine orgasms, but I think that's all delusion, like rehearsed memories of childhood. I know I loved sex, but I believe what I miss is the touching, the movement, the air around it, like I said. The fire notwithstanding. I have these nurses. I know their names from their chatting with each other. There are three women and two men and they are, I believe, kind to me. Emilia, Lauretta, and Elissa see to me during the day and overnight my bags are emptied by Pan and Dion. They are my Pentameron and I listen to them tell their stories every night. They all speak to me, but only one question is common between them. They ask, to a person, Is there anyone in there? I answer, Yes, we are here, we are here. All of us are in here. Nat is still working away on his confessions of Billy Styron, specifically the part where young Billy spies the poor young black daughter of his family's maid and he thinks that she is like bubbles floating in an immediate effulgence of perfection and maybe purity, watching her pause to look up from her work and let her slender brown fingers pass lightly over her damp brow, but at any rate she fills him with a raw kind of hunger, which he chooses to see as a refined, cultivated lust, a well-mannered biological urge. Finally, he pins her behind the foaling shed and *talks* her into having sex with him, but he can't get it up and so he is left to masturbate. It's only fair, Nat says, it's only fair that I too get to tell what is true, what is true, the bison's in the meadow, the elephant's in the zoo. And Murphy and Lang, we're all in here, in all our various time zones and dress and dementias. And I am here, too, refusing to, as my father put it, cram for finals. No holy ghost for me, no accepting this one as my lord and savior, my guide and bookie, my plumber and electrician, and what the fuck does that even mean? My savior? Isn't it amazing how many questions one manufactures when in a vegetative state? Other than Texas.

This is a picture of the road that I find myself walking along now. You will note the trees and perhaps you will recognize them and so imagine you know where I am, but you would be wrong. It's okay to be wrong. I used to think that everything was about exposing nonsense in the world. How did that asshole Wittgenstein put it? To move from disguised nonsense to patent nonsense? Well, turns out that's bullshit. I thought for a while that we were supposed to make sense out of nonsense and then I thought that we were supposed to try to turn sense into nonsense and now I know that we're supposed to make sense that sounds like nonsense and then call the sense nonsensical. That's what I think now. I've had a long life of thinking, if not nonsensical things, then particularly useless and annoying things. Like this.

When young I would climb word ladders. Word ladders would get me from *rest* to *trot*, from *hate* to *love*. *Hate, hale, have, lave, love*. And therefore I can get from *hate* to *live*. But here's the thing. *Live* is *evil* spelled backward, but *evil* cannot be changed into any other word. Same is true of *devil*. What's that all about? I start my fucking ladder with *evil* and I can't get a single step up. I'm just saying. *God*

I can turn into *sod, pod, hod,* and even *cod. Good* becomes *food* rather nicely. But *evil.* You wonder why I wonder. Well, I just do. I'm in a fucking coma. How evil is that?

Pretty evil.

My taking notice of this rather odd fact is not a product of my having been freed from the church. As you know, better than anyone, I was never a participant in the spiritual arts. To their credit I doubt they would ever have let me.

This I'll take on faith.

Not bad. I mention this because often when emancipated from the religious handcuffs, people don't go trotting off to rational thought.

No?

No. They embrace every bit of insipid spiritual and psychic nonsense they can find. Crystals and the Cabala and new age voodoo creams and what have you. I guess it's the nature of human beings. People need something to explain the big bad world out there. Not knowing is not acceptable. Now, I'm going to say something profound. Just giving you a bit of warning. I don't want it to be missed. It's only when we can accept our cluelessness about the world that we can approach the manifestation of the inexhaustibility of ignorance and that is art. Did you write that down? Don't bother. If it turns out to be true then it will only negate what I'm trying to say.

No doubt.

Listen, I've spent my whole life trying to make something I don't understand. Now, I'm just trying to make a good coma. And *coma* spelled backward is *amoc,* which doesn't mean a damn thing.

When my son was quite young, he loved dirt roads. We would be driving through northern Virginia, maybe to visit nurseries looking for roses, maybe just driving to enjoy the autumn foliage, but when he saw a dirt lane, he would sit up and bark, Dirt road, dirt road. Often I would take it and he squealed with delight as

the ruts and rocks bounced our station wagon wildly. Perhaps my
fears were a bit stale, remnants, but I was always worried that we
might come upon a Klan rally or some other miscreant activity.
One night we did. It was dusk, the hour when things become in-
distinct. A magic hour in one's yard, but not so when one was black
and in America's yard. It didn't even seem like fire at first and the
moving figures didn't really appear as men. They didn't make me
think of ghosts or even of anything that should not have been in
woods, but they were there and they were men and they were clad
in white sheets and they did have pointy heads and bad intentions.
Dusk turned abruptly to night and the only lights were from car
headlights behind us, car taillights in front of us, and the waving
of flashlights and lanterns to our sides. The cross was a fire and I
suppose it should have been. The pointy heads were stopping cars,
shining lights into faces and peeking into backseats. I know my son
did not see me reach under the seat to get it, but he saw it quickly
enough, my .32-caliber revolver in my lap, between my legs, what
so many black men kept under their seats for such occasions. When
our turn at the checkpoint came, I stepped on the gas and we fish-
tailed away. We were not chased. The familiar dirt lane led us back
to the main highway, I stuck the pistol back in its home, and we
said nothing, father and son, quietly sharing America. But it could
have happened differently, leaving you a bit of business to tend
to, deal with, sort out. When I stepped on the gas, I slammed into
the baby-blue Chevy pickup that had started across the road. We
lurched forward, your ten-year-old arms catching you against the
dash, my chest thrown into the steering wheel, sounding the horn,
and all of a sudden we were in a world that was like a book with no
pictures or conversation. Pointy heads moved into our car, grabbed
me, and left you to scramble your way out behind. You were pushed
aside and not gently, mind you, by a woman in a sheet, a fat woman
who smelled of butter and dusty upholstery. There were voices,
many voices, that all sounded alike, but were so distinct that later
each one would come to you in turn, in dreams, nightmares. You

crawled and then found your feet and followed as the men laughed
while they dragged me toward the burning cross, the gasoline
fumes apparently reluctant to burn off. You watched while I said
nothing but told you with my eyes to run, to run fast away. A white
boy, wild eyed and full of madness, came and stood beside you and
you studied him like he was from another planet, another species,
and you knew even then that you were right. A man burned me
with his cigarette around my neck, made a ring around my neck.
You tried to find the stench of your father's burning flesh in the air
but found only the gasoline and now the sour breath of the boy
beside you, his mouth crazily wide open. And then there was dead
silence as a rope was brought out, a sacred and cherished rope that
appeared already stained with blood. A noose was placed over my
head and around my neck and you looked at my eyes and I told you
again to run, run away fast, but you did not. You stood stunned.
You were staring at me. Ain't you gonna say anything, nigger? I did
not speak but kept silent. Such silence keeping required that I had
something to say. *There was a Young Lady of Parma,* I thought, *Whose
conduct grew calmer and calmer; When they said, Are you dumb? She
merely said, Hum! That provoking your Lady of Parma.* And I smiled a
half smile and you understood then to run and you did. I watched
your little legs carry you quickly through the distracted herd. They
put the rope in a tree, a tree that sank its roots deep into everywhere, deep into yesterday, deep into my blood and theirs. It was
a big sycamore and so I knew there must be water someplace and I
hoped it would not impede your progress to the main road; then
I remembered the culvert that allowed the stream to pass under
the road and I sighed some relief as the rope tightened around my
neck and my trousers were pulled down to around my ankles. The
main road was just a two-lane blacktop and in later years you would
drive past the dirt road that would be visible but not accessible and
tell your children that that was where their grandfather had been
hanged, not telling them the part about his testicles being cut from
his body by a serrated but edgeless hunting knife, a fitting meta-

phor for the miscreants perpetrating the act. That I then, you then, I now, could imagine such hell was hell enough. This is not a play with counterfactuals, it is not a play with parallel dimensions, it is a cucumber of a man lying voiceless in a bed of ball bearings trying to find a Virgil so I can fire him and tell him to go to hell. Because, I say this in complete half seriousness, things are not as elementary as they appear, a pretext is never more than a pre-text. You know where I am and I know where you are, the cat's in the kitchen the cow's in the car, the dog said he won't be here by five, but he's never seen a cattle drive.

I ran. In the milky faces I saw the soldiers of My Lai, wide-eyed violent lust-burning gazes, their mouths agape and gap toothed, their voice high registered and pig-squealing with perverted delight, hardly animal but all too certainly human. I ran and I ran along that dirt and gravel lane but turned off, afraid that I would be too easily seen in the twilight, the unfolding moonlit night, my white high-top Converse sneakers promising to give me away. So I cut into the inky woods where I made much noise breaking sticks and brush and being slapped by low branches, but my noise was so much less than their beastly moaning that it hardly mattered. I could see my father's expressionless face telling me to run. I wasn't sure I was being chased, to this day I do not know if those red legs, those rednecked inbred bastards, actually chased me into the night. I remember the hooting of owls, especially when I came to a broken-down footbridge, the water racing over its collapsed middle. I used the structure to support myself as I splashed through the chilly water.

I made my way up a steep embankment to the shadowy blacktop, a stretching, sable ribbon twisting through the darkness, and I ran, not choosing a direction; the direction chose me. A pickup truck caught me in its yellowed headlights and skidded to a stop. I was too tired to run any farther and so remained there, bathed in the sick glow, my hands trembling on my soaked denim knees, my chest heaving. It was not until I saw that the driver was a black man that I started quietly crying, for so many reasons. He approached me cautiously, turned sideways like a crab. I tried hard to say something but could not make a sound. He told me to slow down, called me son and I didn't like that, tried to put a hand on my back. I moved away from his touch. I told him that they were going to kill my father, that they were killing him. I said KKK and he scooped me up in his arms, shoved me into the cab of his truck, and drove off in the opposite direction. I recall that the cab of that truck stank of turpentine and that there was no door on the glove compartment.

The stories we could have told. Give me your evidence. Shant, said the cook. And here we are, supine, what a lovely word, like the name of a flower, look at the supines in the meadow, a sad vision actual, a virtual vegetable garden, and we cucumbers among them, in our proper rows. You can be Murphy this time. I'll be you.

Do you see what I see? Turn about and wheel about, and do just so. But all that disappears into the water that is behind us and in the desert that lies ahead. None of what mattered matters and it will not matter if the matter matters, no matter what, as a matter of fact. A lie we would do well to believe. But here I am, me again, head propped up, sort of, at a seventeen-degree angle, the bright overhead lights offering no bother. I could be writing you could be writing me could be writing you. I am a comatose old man writing here now and again what my dead or living son might write if he wrote or I am a dead or living son writing what my dying father might write for me to have written. I am a performative utterance. I carry the illocutionary ax. But imagine anyway that it is as simple as this: I lay dying. My skin used to be darker. Now, I am sallow, wan, icteric. I am not quite bloodless, but that is coming. I can hear the whistle on the tracks. I can also hear screaming, but it is no one I know. So, fuck them.

First Continuation

In some woods you became lost, the darkness swallowed you and then spat you out in a quiet place at dawn, where you sat cross-legged beside a tree that in stories might have been called stalwart or majestic, and you sat in a crook of that massive trunk, where-upon you were approached by a young woman who saw and attended to the wounds on your arms from the brush and thicket, dabbed at your blood with broad leaves from a nearby shrub. She wouldn't look directly at, but stole peeks at, your eyes and you were pleased she was there but more confused, her tender touch slowing your breathing, relaxing your neck. She felt immediately like a friend, steady, redoubtable, like the oak against which you leaned. You wanted to say something, to tell her why you had been running, to ask her how you had come to be in this place, to ask just who she was, but every time you tried to speak kaks and clucks came out and spittle rolled down your chin. The girl finally looked at you and she said, Take care of the sense and the sounds will take care of themselves. Her words were familiar and had the ring of truth, looked true on her lips.

They killed my father, you said.

She nodded sadly. And yet here you are.

And where is that?

Where is what?

Where is here?

It's here.

You sat up straighter and imagined that you understood. What is here next to?

There.

And how far is it from here to there?

Once you leave here, you'll be there. You're silly. Next you'll no doubt want to know how long it takes to get there. Well, I can tell, it varies. If you look over there you'll see that it's here for as far as you can see. Do you hear that?

What?

It's the bear. He's here.

Where?

Over there.

How can he be here and there?

Oh, here and there are not so different. The two are so much more alike than then and now or now and again, but not near as similar as how and why.

How and why? How are they alike?

Why do you ask?

Because you just said that how is like why.

No, I said they are similar.

I know.

You're not suggesting that similar and alike are the same thing, are you? Why, they couldn't be more different.

How are they different?

I don't know. You tell me. I just know that they couldn't be more different. They can't, can they?

I need to find my father.

I thought you said they killed him, whoever *they* is.

The klansmen killed him.

Whoever they are, she said. Back to how and why? You will later ask yourself how you survived and you will wonder why you survived. So you see, one is the other and vice versa.

I don't care about all that. You pushed yourself to your feet and brushed off your clothes, then paused to wonder why you'd bothered. I have to be going, you said. I don't like it here. All you speak is nonsense.

Of course, that's true, and wouldn't it be sad if I didn't? Of course I do and I rhyme, too, but I could make not a sound if it weren't for you.

I'm sad about my father.

You miss him.

Yes.

But imagine if you didn't.

What do you mean?

Imagine what it would mean if you didn't feel so bad, if he were dead and you didn't feel a thing or you felt good.

That's not possible.

It's not possible only because it isn't, but it is very possible because it could be and since it could be, try to imagine what it would mean. When children die they come back as themselves as adults.

What about when adults die?

A riddle, a riddle, violin or fiddle.

Who are you? you asked.

I am a little girl.

What's your name?

My name is Name. My name is my name and the name of both the word *name* and Name, my name. I am not the only one with the name Name and also there are other names.

I'm getting out of here.

Not yet. This voice was not Name's. It came from the thicket behind you. It was deep and throaty, a familiar voice, and it reminded you of a baritone sax. You turned to it and it was someone who looked just like you, unless of course it was you. You looked at the one that looked like you.

Who are you? you asked.

Who are you? the one that looked like you asked.

You look like me.

And you like me.

And your name is?

You. You are my name.

You mean You is your name?

What kind of grammar is that? You are my name?

Shall I call you You?

No, you are my name.

I am your name?

Yes, You.

Spell your name.

How can you be spelled?

Y-O-U.

That spells you? How can a person be spelled?

Are you saying that *I* am your name?

Now you're getting it. You are my name?

Then how shall I call you?

Why would you want to call me?

Name spoke up. What a mess, what a mess. The pig's playing checkers, the cow's playing chess. You are his name.

How can I be his name? I'm not even a word.

Don't sell yourself short, the one who looks like you said. You are as good a name as any.

Do you know him? you asked.

Of course.

And if you wanted to get his attention, what would you call him?

Name pointed at you.

Me?

Name shook her head. Anyway, why would I want to call him when I can call you?

You shook your head. Where are we? you asked.

We're in a coma, the one who looks like you said.

We used to be in a pickle, Name said. And then for a while we were in a comma, but we lost an *m*.

What am I doing in a coma?

Waiting to die, the one who looks like you said.

Why do you look like me?

Why do you look like me?

I am your name?

You are my name?

You?

No, you.

A coma?

A coma.

There once was a man in a coma, who couldn't close up his stoma, the words they fell in, the words they fell out, yet he no longer desired to rhumba. Death is no way to die.

Of course there's nothing after it, the one that looks like you said.

After what? you ask.

After it, he said. I said there is nothing after it and that's where I stopped. There was nothing after it.

It.

Qui.

And after it?

Nada.

Before it? As lingua.

Alles.

Why are you doing that?

What?

Answering in different languages.

Non so cosa vuoi dire?

Like that. French, Spanish, German, and now Italian.

Der er ingen forsskellige sprog.

What the hell is that?

Todas as linguas são a mesma coisa.

Why is he doing this? you ask Name.

Doing what?

Saying these things.

Saying is doing?

What?

Dire est faire.

Stop it.

You are his name.

I am his name?

You are my name.

I have a word for you.

And what is that?

Why, it is a sound that when uttered renders either the understanding of a thing, action, or concept, the smallest unit of meaningful language.

I mean what is the word?

Except when the word is meaningless, and we do say things like that's a made-up word. Which is a way to say that it is no word at all.

What is the word?
Indelible.
Indelible.
Indelible.

The Second Face of Desire

. . . lying here like this I have learned some things about us and learned nothing at all and it is the *nothing at all* that sings to me in this cucumbery trance, that we may assume, we may choose to assume, that as any given state of affairs is upset, that there arises an instinct to make them anew and as we set about we entertain all these words, all these thoughts, notions, utterances, calculations, equations, texts, all of this, and language remains always a step ahead of us, and we think this most clearly as we die, a step, two steps ahead of us, our speaking, our writing, our groping always lags behind language, far enough that there is nothing to say about language itself, as we cannot look directly upon its magnificence, like Semele and Zeus, burn baby burn, and yet, a Hegelian desire, a Freudian instinct, no matter how much we yak, how much we entangle ourselves in words and texts, all we ever do is circle where we think language might reside, guessing like we guess about the location of electrons, about positrons and pions and muons and kaons and leptons and quarks and imaginary ducks, using it without pause, without thought, knowing that we cannot live without it, that we define ourselves with it and by it, but it is not ours, it found us, waited for us to find it, we evolved to find it waiting and we explore its structure, the structure we impose, believe we add to its content daily, recognize its turns, its fluidity, its features, its alterability, and yet we cannot account for it, explain it, find the egg of it, because it is, in short, god, the only god that we know or will know or have known, it being immaterial, without form or mass or weight or constituent parts, the identification of parts of speech being little more than an exercise in question begging, like describing judgments by examples of things judged, and it is completely dependent on us and yet we give it nothing, just as digging more ditch makes the ditch no more a ditch and it dies every day and yet continues to live, lives in units that we cannot see or hear and so big that we cannot miss them and we can represent none of them, as it exists without senses, without medium, without intention, without reflection or deflection, but not without us, as it makes us human, forces us to be human, reminds us to be human, yet has no feeling toward us, gives us life, conflict, confusion, war, and understanding, and it is all-powerful and without judgment and it can state its own apparent inadequacy and then overcome it, revealing that we are the site of the failure, create contexts, is contexts, is not the sum of its parts, and we cannot see, imagine, the whole of it, cannot imagine it at all and it creates gods for us to pray to, gods for us to fear and love, creates religions and then refutes them, creates a way for us to talk about the unknown, about language itself and yet does not create itself, is not created, just is, and we cannot imagine ourselves without it, cannot imagine without it, because it is god and it lets us know that god is just a word, that god is just a grammar, that its grammar is just our feeble construct to approach its radiance, it has nothing to do with texts, it has nothing to do with words, and probably has nothing to do with our thoughts and the things we think when we know we know nothing when we know there is nothing when nothing is our last safe cave of language, and vegetable, vegetable, vegetable me, the sky's in the river, the moon's in the sea, the birds speak in riddles and the dolphins tell lies, that we'll all live forever and that nobody dies . . .

So, As I Was Saying

I was not so different from the way I ever was except that everyone considered me to be on the other side of consciousness. That previous sentence could have been rendered in present tense, but that would hardly have made it present. I was dead the day I was born or at least headed toward death and I must say that I stayed the course with rather impressive and also rather common tenacity.

One follows one and the other follows another and finally it doesn't matter who died when or how or where. So do not bury my ashes in an urn, I said to them every hour, and I imagined that they of course did not hear me. But put my ashes loose on the ground, in a broad shallow ditch where I might feed something, what planet there is left. Say nothing over what was me, just sprinkle me, I said. Maybe even put a small bit of me here and a smidgen of me over there. Just spread me about. But for devil's sake, don't set me on a table and pretend to converse with me, I said. And so it was.

I Keep My Doubts in a Box with the Things I Know

I listened to her with great attention. I wanted to know exactly what she meant. She was saying something about Ottawa and a pilot and it all sounded like a jumble, but one of those particularly important jumbles, the kind one both wants and doesn't want to hear. And so I listened with great interest and desire to have it be of no significance. But you know how it goes. Significance abounded. There was more significance than I could shake a stick at. I did shake a stick, in my fashion.

I slept with him, she said.

Sleeping was not such a bad thing, I thought. Not much happens when asleep, but I of course understood and supplied the response she no doubt expected, wanted, and needed. I said, What the fuck?

Despite my education, profession, and disposition, that was all I could come up with. I was disappointed, but only as a means to feel something other than hurt, fear, shame, and any number of ugly and unflattering things. I recognized, even then, in my tarantella of overanalysis, that I had made the whole matter about me and at once was ignoring and acknowledging why she might have seen fit to *sleep* with someone else in the first place. So I said, I'm sorry.

And with that you stole away my mother's moment. She went rigid, froze in the headlights of your apparent, seeming understanding. Your self-absorbed act of compassion, your unthinking gesture of solicitude, left her without a portal to reasonable outrage, indignation, or guilt. I'm sorry, you said.

I sat on the stairs, that standard cliché sitting place for a child listening to a parental argument. Even at thirteen I understood that you had usurped her power, taken away her position of hurter and abandoned your part as victim. Yet you managed to maintain the dance of being victimized while reducing her action to a mere response to your influence on her life. It was swift, deft, and finally cruel. And the worst of it was that you seemed oblivious to your own diabolical genius, but then I knew you couldn't be unaware or incognizant, believed that you were too smart to not see what you were doing. Knowing that you were not evil, I came to believe that you were deluded. You'd convinced yourself that you were behaving nobly, showing kindness of a sort, acting magnanimously.

She had delivered her news to you in the morning. The sun had etched grooves of daylight through the window and across the wide-boarded wooden floor of the farmhouse kitchen. She turned her back to you and let the light strike her front.

Surely, you have something to say, you said.

That was when she spied me, still in my cotton pajamas, perched on the stairs. She spoke to you without taking her never-more-beautiful eyes from me. It won't happen again, she said.

Then you saw me and no doubt you saw in my eyes my anger with you and you tried to make the necessary shift, tried to return her to her rightful role in the play. You began to cry.

She turned to you and held you while you sat at the kitchen table. She comforted you and while she did I caught you peeking to see if I was still there, then you returned quickly to your business, surprised to have found me. Watching you cry for her restored my faith in you, made me smarter. I knew that you were really hurt by what she had told you, but I also knew that hurt you displayed was completely artificial, manufactured for her and maybe just a little for me.

Cold Are the Crabs That Crawl on Yonder Hills

For you, by me, or for me, by you. The water is high and the mountain is blue. The children are screaming there's nothing to do while the rain falls on many, but not on the few. I'm lightly sautéed with butter and thyme, turned over twice but never in time. The flame that you cook on is blue at its core. It's hot, yes, it's hot, but it will burn me no more. I'm there then I'm here. I'm near then I'm far. It's too far for our legs; it's too near for the car. The hills are too flat and the plains are too steep; the water's too hard and the rocks are too deep. You loved me on Monday and on Wednesday again and up in the mountains but not on the fen.

Cold Are the Cucumbers That Crawl Beneath

Cucumber, I. Twitch a finger here. Twitch a finger there. Fuck with them any way you can. I'm dead, but they don't know it. Forget the adage let sleeping dogs lie. How about we let dead men die?

You hold my hand.

I hold your hand.

I write this for you.

If I wrote, this would be it.

If you wrote.

Yes.

I will always be here.

And I.

I'm dead, son.

I know that, Dad. But I didn't know you knew it.

PERCIVAL EVERETT is Distinguished Professor of English at the University of Southern California and the author of more than thirty books, including *Dr. No, The Trees, Telephone, I Am Not Sidney Poitier*, and *Erasure*.

Percival Everett by Virgil Russell has been typeset in Dante, a font created by Giovanni Mardersteig and Charles Malin in the mid-1950s. Design and composition by BookMobile Design and Digital Publisher Services, Minneapolis, Minnesota. Manufactured by Versa Press on acid-free 30 percent postconsumer wastepaper.